"You could have been killed."

Her voice was strained, barely a whisper, but he heard the emotions loud and clear.

That wasn't ordinary concern for a fellow human being. That was concern for her baby's daddy. Maybe even for him.

It only added another layer of complications to their already complicated situation.

Kendall was pregnant with his baby. They were a Texas version of Romeo and Juliet. Star-crossed lovers. And since that story hadn't had a happy ending, this extra layer only made him worry more.

He'd clearly developed a fondness for complicated layers. Apparently, a fondness for having Kendall in his arms, too.

"I'm sorry," he whispered.

"For what?"

"Everything."

Kendall stared at him, those eyes so green that they looked like spring itself. Spring with heat, of course. Even now the heat was there.

SURRENDERING TO THE SHERIFF

USA TODAY Bestselling Author

DELORES FOSSEN

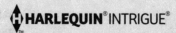

Recycling programs
for this product may
not exist in your area.

ISBN-13: 978-0-373-69842-4

Surrendering to the Sheriff

Copyright © 2015 by Delores Fossen

Printed in U.S.A.

Delores Fossen, a *USA TODAY* bestselling author, has sold over fifty novels with millions of copies of her books in print worldwide. She's received the Booksellers' Best Award and the RT Reviewers' Choice Award, and was a finalist for a prestigious RITA® Award. You can contact the author through her webpage at dfossen.net.

Books by Delores Fossen

HARLEQUIN INTRIGUE

Sweetwater Ranch series

Maverick Sheriff
Cowboy Behind the Badge
Rustling Up Trouble
Kidnapping in Kendall County
The Deputy's Redemption
Reining in Justice
Surrendering to the Sheriff

The Lawmen of Silver Creek Ranch series

Grayson
Dade
Nate
Kade
Gage
Mason
Josh
Sawyer

Visit the Author Profile page
at Harlequin.com for more titles.

CAST OF CHARACTERS

Sheriff Aiden Braddock—When two men kidnap his former flame Kendall O'Neal, Aiden comes face-to-face not only with old dangers from the past, but also a new secret that could tear his family apart.

Kendall O'Neal—For years she's tried to avoid Aiden because of their family feud, but a one-night stand brings the past to a head and ends up threatening both of their lives.

Carla Braddock—Aiden's mother. She's very bitter about Aiden and Kendall's relationship, but how far would she go to stop it?

Jewell O'Neal—Kendall's half sister who's in jail awaiting trial for murdering Aiden's father. She's the reason the Braddocks and the O'Neals are locked in a fierce family feud.

Lee Palmer—A wealthy rancher who had plenty of bad blood with Aiden's family, but he also has some secrets. Those secrets could be the reason Kendall and Aiden are now in danger.

Robert Joplin—Jewell's lawyer. He's in love with Jewell and would do anything to clear her name. That might include risking Kendall's life to destroy evidence that could incriminate Jewell.

FBI Agent Seth Calder—Jewell's stepson. He's very protective of Jewell and Kendall and doesn't trust the Braddocks.

Chapter One

Sheriff Aiden Braddock shut the door behind him, tossed his truck keys on the kitchen counter.

And stopped cold.

He didn't hear anything unusual. The whir of the A/C and fridge. The April breeze rattling the oaks outside the window over the sink. All the sounds he should be hearing, but he still got the gut feeling that something wasn't right.

Since that gut feeling had saved his butt a time or two during his time as county sheriff, Aiden listened to it.

He drew his Glock from his holster.

Aiden didn't move yet. He just stood there a few more moments. Listening. And then he heard the thing that didn't belong. A whisper, maybe. Or somebody breathing. Because he lived alone, there darn sure shouldn't be anyone else whispering or breathing in his house.

"Mom?" Aiden called out just to make sure. Though it'd been longer than a blue moon since she came out to his place. Too far in the sticks, she had always complained.

"Laine? Shelby?" Aiden added in case it was one of his sisters. Again, a serious long shot, since they rarely visited, either.

No answer. But he hadn't expected one.

Whatever was going on, this likely wasn't a social visit and could even involve some attempted bodily harm. After all, he was the county sheriff and had riled more than a person or two over the past decade. One of those riled people had perhaps come to settle an old score.

Aiden huffed. He was so not in the mood to bash some heads, but he might have to do just that.

"Let's make this easy for you," Aiden called out. "I'm a damn good shot. Plus, I'm hungry, tired and not feeling up to any idiot who's stupid enough to break into a lawman's house."

"Aiden," someone said in a hoarse whisper.

Even though the person hardly made any sound when she spoke, Aiden thought he recognized the voice.

Kendall.

But that didn't make any sense. This was the last place on earth she'd come.

Especially after…well, just *after.*

Aiden didn't lower his gun, but he inched his way toward the sound of her whisper—in his living room. It was just a few yards away past a half wall, but he kept watch all around him. Kept listening, too. Until he could move into the arched opening that divided the rooms, and he snapped his gun in the direction where he'd pinpointed Kendall's voice.

His heart slammed against his chest.

Because it was Kendall O'Neal all right, but this definitely wasn't a social visit. She was on her knees in the center of the floor, and there was a hulking man on each side of her. The men were wearing black ski masks, and both had automatics pointed right at her head.

"Drop the gun, Sheriff Braddock," the bigger one on the right growled.

Aiden held on to his Glock, trying to figure out what

the devil was going on here. He didn't get many clues from Kendall. She only shook her head. Like an apology or something.

But that was pure fear in her wide eyes.

He didn't see any signs of injury, but then most of her body that he could see was covered with a pale blue shirt, skirt and business jacket—her lawyering clothes. However, her hair was a mess, her blond locks tangled on her shoulders.

So maybe she'd been in a scuffle with these guys after all.

Kendall wasn't the messy-hair type. Nope. All priss and polish for her and never a hair out of place. People didn't call her the ice princess for nothing.

However, that wasn't an ice-princess look she was giving him now.

"What do you want?" Aiden asked the men.

"Your gun on the floor." Again, it was the one on the right who answered. No unusual accent. He was a Texan. And the nondescript dark pants and T-shirt didn't give Aiden any clues, either.

"Do it *now*," the man added, and he jammed his gun against Kendall's head. "Or else she'll pay the price."

The last thing any lawman wanted to do was surrender his weapon, but Aiden was wearing his usual backup gun in a boot holster. Maybe he'd be able to get to it in time if things turned uglier than they already were.

Of course, things were already plenty ugly enough.

Aiden didn't make any fast moves. He eased his gun onto the floor. "Now, what's this about?" he demanded. Thankfully, he still sounded like a sheriff even though it was hard to sound badass and in charge with guns pointed at Kendall.

"You're going to do us a favor," the gunman said. Even

though the ski mask covered most of the gunman's face, Aiden could have sworn the guy was smirking. "And if you don't, then we'll hurt Kendall here. Won't kill her at first. But we'll use her to make sure you cooperate."

The threat was real enough—the *real* guns were proof of that—but Aiden had to shake his head. "You do know that Kendall O'Neal and I aren't exactly on speaking terms, right? Everybody in town knows it. So why use her to get me to do anything for you?"

But his question ground to a halt, and Aiden's gaze snapped back to her.

"This is some kind of sick game, isn't it?" Though he couldn't imagine why Kendall would be playing it with these two armed thugs. "Is this connected to your sister?"

Aiden didn't wait for an answer. His attention went back to her captors. If they were indeed linked to her sister and not paid help trying to trick him into doing something crazier than what they were already doing.

"Just in case you don't know," Aiden told the men, "Kendall's half sister, Jewell, is about to stand trial for murdering my father twenty-three years ago. If this was a real hostage situation, you'd have taken someone that I actually care a rat's you know what about."

Kendall flinched at his stinging remark, but she quickly recovered. The fear, or fake fear, was still in her green cat eyes, and she hiked up her chin in that way that always riled him to the core. She looked darn haughty when she did that.

"There are things you don't know." Her voice cracked on the last word. A nice, theatrical touch.

"Clearly," Aiden said with a boatload of sarcasm. "But let me guess. You're a thousand steps past the desperate stage, and you'd do anything to save your precious, murdering sister. So you want me to try to fix the trial or something."

Aiden rammed his thumb against his chest and had to finish through clenched teeth. "You picked the wrong mark, Kendall. I don't break the law for anybody, especially the likes of you."

And he got another lightbulb moment.

A very bad one. One brought on by the *likes of you* comment. It hadn't been that long ago that he said those very words to her.

Not in the heat of the moment like now.

More like *after* the heat.

Yeah, Kendall and he had had the hots for each other since middle school. Forbidden fruit and all that crap. Aiden had always resisted her because he'd known it would tear his family apart.

Until three months ago.

He'd had to kill a man that day. A domestic disturbance gone wrong. Then he'd had a run-in with his mother. Then another run-in with one of Jewell's smart-mouthed daughters. To make matters worse, he'd dropped by the Bluebonnet for a drink or two. Which had turned into four. All right, five.

And he'd run into Kendall.

Aiden hadn't asked her what kind of bad day she'd been trying to erase with those shots of high-end whiskey she was downing like water. But the drinks had dumbed him down just enough that he'd gone over to talk to her. A mistake.

A big one.

Because the next thing Aiden knew, they were doing more than talking. They'd landed in bed for some drunken sex, and he'd committed one of the worst mistakes he could ever have made.

Did that night play a part in this, too?

Aiden hadn't been very nice to her the next morning what with his hangover and regret. That was where the *likes of you* comment had come into play. Because he'd wanted to leave immediately, find a big rock and hit himself in the head with it. But maybe Kendall thought she was a woman scorned, and paired with her obsession to clear her sister's name, perhaps the desperation had spilled over to this.

"Get out," Aiden ordered them, and he reached down to pick up his gun.

Aiden didn't get far before the shot blasted through the room and sent his ears ringing. The bullet hadn't been aimed at him.

But rather at Kendall.

She screamed out in pain. Not a whimper, but a full-fledged, blood-chilling scream. For a good reason, too. The bullet had gone into her arm, tearing through her jacket sleeve and into her flesh.

Almost immediately, a bright red patch of blood started to spread over the fabric. She struggled, trying to clamp her hand over it, but he realized then that her wrists had been bound behind her back with plastic cuffs.

Aiden's instincts were to rush to her, to make sure she was okay. He would have done that for anyone. But when he started toward her, the guy on the left shifted his gun to Aiden.

"Move and she gets another bullet in the other arm," the man warned him.

Okay. So maybe this wasn't fake after all.

"You've got my attention," Aiden said. "But let's hurry along this little chat so I can get an ambulance out here for Kendall."

The talking guy shook his head. "Her injury isn't serious. Just a flesh wound. That doesn't mean the next one will be, though. We need her alive but not necessarily in one piece."

Aiden's heartbeat hadn't settled down since he first saw Kendall kneeling on the floor, and that didn't do much to slow it to normal.

"What do you want?" Aiden repeated.

"For you to destroy evidence lot BR6847-23." The guy didn't hesitate.

Normally, Aiden wouldn't have known what evidence that was. But he did in this case. It was recently found bone fragments.

His father's bone fragments.

And it was key evidence in the murder case against Jewell.

"So this is about your sister," he said to Kendall. Even though he no longer believed Kendall had orchestrated it. Not after taking that bullet.

She moaned, the sound of raw pain, and clamped her teeth over her bottom lip for a moment. "I don't know who hired these men," Kendall said, her voice shaking. "I was leaving work late, and they grabbed me in the parking lot. They brought me here."

Even though there weren't a lot of details in that, Aiden could almost see it, and it turned his stomach a little. Kendall wasn't a large woman, and these two goons towered over her. She had to have been terrified.

Still was.

No one was that good an actor.

"Jewell's daughters could be behind this," Aiden said just to see what kind of reaction he'd get from them. No one argued. But then, he didn't see anything in their body language that he'd hit a home run, either.

Of course, who else would it be?

Jewell had abandoned her husband and three sons all those years ago when she left town under the cloud of suspicion of murdering Aiden's father. The suspicion had finally been confirmed when the case was reopened, and those bone fragments had been discovered. Jewell was finally where she belonged.

In jail.

And she hadn't exactly mended fences with her own sons and ex-husband.

Still, she had two daughters, a stepson and a now-shot half sister on her side. Once Kendall was safe, Aiden would go to Jewell's spawn and step-spawn and demand answers.

First, though, he had to get Kendall out of this.

"I guess you'll hold her until I destroy the evidence?" Aiden asked.

The talker nodded. "The sooner you do it, the sooner you can have her back."

Not likely.

Except that didn't make sense, either. Jewell's kids knew she loved her much younger half sister. In fact, word was that Jewell thought of Kendall more like a daughter than a half sister.

So why would Jewell's kids have put Kendall at risk like this?

"Why?" Aiden repeated out loud and shook his head. "And that *why* covers a lot of territory. There's plenty about this that doesn't make sense."

Kendall opened her mouth. Closed it. Then swallowed hard. "I thought Laine might have said something."

Aiden shook his head. "My sister? What does she have to do with this?"

"Laine saw me coming out of the doctor's office. I swear, Aiden, I was going to leave town next week. I wasn't going to put any of this on you. I know how you and your family feel about me."

There was a gun trained on him, but Aiden went some steps closer so he could look Kendall straight in the eye. "What the heck are you talking about?"

She made a sound. Sort of a helpless moan that came from deep within her chest. "They took me because I'm pregnant. Because they knew they could use that for leverage."

Kendall's breath shuddered. "Aiden, the baby I'm carrying is yours."

Chapter Two

It was hard to think through the pain, but Kendall braced herself for Aiden's reaction. She expected him to curse or yell. To ask what she'd already asked herself—how could this have happened? But other than a few moments of silence, that was it.

Those moments of silence were his only physical response to the baby.

Unlike her.

She was sweating now. Not because it was hot but because her arm was throbbing. Yes, it was just a flesh wound, but she was bleeding, and she needed the wound cleaned and tended. Later, if there was a later, she'd deal with Aiden's reaction.

Heaven knew what that would be.

"How do you think this is going to work?" Aiden's attention shifted from her to the gunman who'd been doing all the talking.

"You'll leave now. Go to the evidence storage room. You shouldn't have any trouble getting in there, since you're the county sheriff. Tell them you need to look at something else that involves another case. And once you're inside, destroy the evidence."

Aiden shook his head. "It won't be that simple. There are surveillance cameras."

"Then figure out a way around them," the gunman snapped. "After all, your kid's life depends on it."

Now Aiden cursed, but it was under his breath. "And what about Kendall? You shot her. It can't be good for my *kid* to have his or her mother injured like that."

"Don't worry about her. We'll get her to a doctor. The only thing you have to worry about is doing what you've been told." The man took something from his shirt pocket and tossed it to Aiden.

A cell phone.

"It'll take videos," he explained. "Film yourself destroying the evidence and send it to the number already programmed into the phone."

"And then you'll let Kendall go?" Aiden asked with plenty of skepticism in his tone.

"Eventually. In a day or two. We got no reason to keep her, and truth is, she's a pain in the butt. I, for one, will be glad to give her back to you. She bit me," he growled, glancing down at his wrist.

She had indeed resorted to biting and clawing. She'd done everything to try to escape. But when he threatened to hurt the baby, Kendall knew she had no choice but to stop fighting and look for a better way out of this.

So far, she hadn't come up with one.

This definitely didn't qualify as *better*.

"Hate to burst your bubble," Aiden said, "but if you hold Kendall for a day or two, someone will report her missing. And people will look for her. You really want to raise those kinds of red flags, since half of her kin are lawmen?"

Kendall groaned softly. "I've already told my friends, Jewell and the rest of my family that I'd be leaving town tomorrow morning. I said I needed some downtime and for them not to be surprised if they didn't hear from me for a while."

The gunman laughed. "She tied it up in a pretty little bow for us, didn't she?"

Yes, she did, but Kendall intended to shove that proverbial bow down his throat the first chance she got. She wasn't in any position to win a physical fight with him, but sooner or later, he'd let down his guard.

She hoped.

Aiden's gaze came back to her. "I'm figuring you didn't ask to be here, but I know you won't shed any tears over this evidence being destroyed."

"You're wrong," she let him know after she choked back another wave of pain. "I don't want my sister convicted of murder, but I don't want her free like this, either. And neither would Jewell."

The corner of Aiden's mouth lifted in an expression she knew all too well. The Braddock smirk. As an O'Neal and Jewell's sister, she'd been on the receiving end of it a lot since their families were at odds for twenty-three years.

"Time for you to leave," the gunman said to Aiden. "Oh, and don't bother to pull some kind of stunt like pretending to leave so you can double back and rescue her. Kendall will be tucked away someplace safe, where you can't find her."

There was no telling what they'd consider someplace safe, but she seriously doubted these snakes had her safety in mind beyond using her to try to prod Aiden into committing a felony.

Aiden stood there, his glare shifting among them, and he cursed again. "Give me at least two hours, and you'll have your video of me destroying the bone fragments."

Oh, mercy. He was going to do it.

Kendall had thought he'd be able to negotiate his way out of this. Or else fight his way out of it. She figured the last thing on earth Aiden would do was destroy evidence to protect her.

Except it was not just her.

Even though they were enemies, she knew that Aiden was an honorable man. He wouldn't risk an unborn child's life.

Any unborn child.

Still, honor aside, he'd have a heck of a time dealing with the consequences. And worse. Kendall was terrified that destroying the evidence wouldn't even help the baby and her. She hadn't seen either of the men's faces. Had no idea who they were. But they might not let her live anyway.

The thought of it broke her heart.

Not for her own life but for the baby's. This child hadn't been planned. Heck, it hadn't even been on her personal radar. But she'd loved the baby from the moment that she'd known she was carrying it. However, she never expected Aiden would feel the same.

Ever.

"Get her to the doctor," Aiden growled. *"Now."* And he reached for his gun.

"Nope," the man said while Aiden was in mid-reach. "I'm sure you'll have no trouble coming up with another one. We'll keep this one for now."

Kendall's imagination started to run wild. Once Aiden had destroyed the evidence, they wouldn't have a reason to keep her alive. They could use Aiden's gun to kill her and then somehow set him up to take the blame for the crime.

The baby would be motive.

Because an autopsy would reveal the pregnancy, and a DNA test would prove he was the child's father. These men could make it look as if Aiden had completely lost it when he learned of the baby and killed her in cold blood.

"Oh, and, Braddock?" the man said to Aiden. "We'll know if you call your buddies at the county sheriff's office. Or any other law enforcement agency in the area for that matter. Because we've got *ears* in all those places."

That was probably a bluff. Unless, of course, these guys had managed to plant some listening devices.

"Aiden," she said before she could stop herself. Kendall hated to beg for his help, but she would. To save the baby, she'd do anything.

A flash of something went through his eyes, but Kendall had no idea what it meant. Aiden gave the men, and her, one last look before he strolled out.

Kendall tried to tamp down the panic. They wouldn't kill her until they were sure Aiden had destroyed the evidence, and he'd said that would take about two hours. Not much time. But during those two hours, she had to find a way to escape.

One of the men stayed next to her, the gun still pointed at her head, and the other went to the window and peered out. Watching Aiden, no doubt.

Another sound only spiked the panic building inside her.

Aiden's truck engine.

She heard it start, and then he pulled away from the house.

His place wasn't that large by Texas standards, just a couple of acres of pasture for his horses, a barn and the house. From the man's vantage point at the window, he would be able not only to see Aiden leave, but also to see him drive out onto the road.

"He's out of sight," the man said a moment later.

Still, they didn't move. The time seemed to crawl by,

and her throbbing arm and building panic didn't help. Finally, the one who'd been silent latched on to her shoulder and hauled her to her feet.

"Don't do anything stupid," the other one snarled, "or you'll get another bullet."

Kendall was positive that wasn't a bluff, but before this ordeal was over, she would almost certainly have to do something *stupid*. Or at least risky.

As soon as they started moving, she tried to work the plastic cuffs that bound her wrists behind her back. They were loose, but strong for mere plastic, and they seemed to tighten with each tug.

Those tugs also didn't help the jolts of pain going through her arm. And the pain didn't help the dizziness. She'd been light-headed since this whole ordeal started, but it was more than just a light head now.

The gunshot and the fear were no doubt to blame.

Kendall drew in several hard breaths and forced herself to look down at the wound. At the gaping hole in her jacket. It turned her stomach, but she tried to make sure she wasn't bleeding out.

She wasn't.

There was blood all right, but there didn't seem to be much more than when he'd initially shot her. That was something at least. A serious blood loss could cause her to miscarry.

The men finally led her out the front door, the same way they'd brought her in after one of them had jimmied the lock. Aiden had a security system, but it hadn't been on. He probably hadn't felt the need because he was the sheriff.

Too bad.

If the system had been armed, Aiden might have been alerted and could have nipped this in the bud.

They went onto the porch, down the steps and through the yard toward a thick cluster of trees to the right where the men had left the SUV they'd used to kidnap her from the parking lot of her law office. After they'd grabbed her, they'd stopped several miles outside town to change the license plates and to make a call. Kendall hadn't learned a thing from that call, because they'd said only one thing to the person on the other end of the line.

"We have her."

No names used. No hint of the identity of the person they'd called.

So, who had put all this insanity into motion?

Despite Aiden's accusations and suspicions, it wasn't Jewell or her daughters. Not Jewell's stepson, Seth, either. Yes, the three of them loved Jewell, but they wouldn't resort to this. Unfortunately, other than those three children, Kendall and Jewell's lawyer, Robert Joplin, there weren't many people who wanted Jewell to beat this murder charge.

But clearly someone wanted just that.

When they were about ten yards from the SUV, Kendall stumbled just to see how fast the men would react, and she got her answer.

Fast.

Both of them grabbed her, and within a second, she had a gun jammed against her left temple again.

"Keep it up, and you'll be sorry," one of the men growled.

No matter what she did, she could be sorry, but Kendall cooperated.

For now.

She continued toward the SUV and didn't resist when the men practically shoved her inside. As they'd done on the drive there, they buckled her into a seat belt in the middle, and the man who'd spoken only a few words dropped down behind her. The one who'd been doing all the talking walked around the front of the SUV toward the driver's side.

But then he stopped.

That certainly got her attention, but it got his partner's, too. "What's wrong?" the man asked. Unlike the other one, he had some kind of thick accent.

The man still outside raised his finger in a wait-a-second gesture and lifted his head. Listening for something.

Or maybe *someone.*

Kendall hoped and prayed that it was someone who could get her away from these goons.

"Don't move," the guy with the accent said to her, and he stepped out of the SUV. Not far. Just a few inches outside the open door, and he, too, listened. His gaze also darted all around the heavily treed area.

Kendall looked, as well. She tried to pick through the trees and underbrush, but it was spring with everything in full bloom, so she couldn't see anything.

However, she thought that she might have heard something, like a twig snap. The men didn't miss it. With their guns raised, they pivoted in the direction of the sound.

Again, nothing.

For several seconds anyway.

Then the shot zinged through the air. It hadn't been fired by one of her captors but had instead come from the area of that dense underbrush.

It had to be Aiden.

He would have known to cut through the woods and come back after them.

Her captors immediately lifted their guns to return fire, and Kendall sank down into the seat as far as she could. She also looked for something, anything, she could use to cut through the plastic cuffs.

Outside, both men fired, their bullets blasting through the air. She quickly added another prayer that Aiden hadn't been shot.

Both men continued to fire. Kendall continued to struggle, and even though it made the pain in her arm much worse, she managed to move her hand so she could pop the button on the seat belt. It slid off her, and she got to the floor. Not just for protection but so she could look under the seat.

There was a first aid kit.

She fumbled through it as best she could and found a pair of scissors. They were small, the kind used for cutting bandages and not restraints. Still, they would have to do.

It was hard enough just to pick them up with her hands behind her back. Harder still to try to make any cut. But she had to try.

Kendall glanced out. Both men were now at the front of the SUV and they were tearing up the woods with their bullets. Even though Aiden's nearest neighbor was a half mile away, maybe he would hear the noise and report it if Aiden hadn't already called for backup.

The man with the accent looked into the SUV. His gaze connected with hers through the gap between the front seats, and he said something to his partner that she couldn't hear. But the man must have realized she was trying to escape, because he hurried toward the driver's door.

Coming for her.

Her heart was pumping now. The adrenaline, too. Kendall worked even harder at trying to cut through the plastic. She could feel them giving way. Little by little. But the man was practically right on her.

The plastic cuffs gave way, finally.

Just as the man crawled across the seat and grabbed for her.

But Kendall brought up the scissors and stabbed him in the face. Because of the ski mask, she wasn't sure what part of him she hit, but he howled in pain and came at her.

Kendall hit him again with the scissors. This time in his neck.

He made some kind of strangled sound, and she saw the blood. Nothing like her gunshot wound. There was lots of it, and the agonizing sound that he made sent his partner running to him.

Kendall knew she had mere seconds at best. The side door was already open, and she barreled through it. She hadn't realized just how dizzy and weak she was until her feet touched the ground.

Everything started to spin.

And she would no doubt have fallen if someone hadn't caught her by the arm. She could just barely make out Aiden's face.

"Come on," Aiden said.

He turned, fired a shot at the men, and then he and Kendall started running.

Chapter Three

Aiden pulled Kendall behind the nearest tree, shoving her against it so that he could lean out and try to stop these guys from coming after them.

And they were coming all right.

Well, one of them anyway.

The other one had his hand clamped to his neck and was slumped against the SUV. Aiden hoped that whatever the heck his injury was, it would kill him. Harsh, yes, but maybe necessary for Kendall's and his survival. One armed man was enough to deal with, considering that he had an injured, pregnant woman to rescue.

Pregnant.

That one little word came with a boatload of emotions attached and packed a wallop. Especially since Kendall was the one who was pregnant.

With his baby, no less.

That sounded about as unright as something could sound, but he had indeed slept with her. He'd also used protection. However, something had clearly gone wrong other than them just landing in bed together.

Fate had to be laughing its butt off about that. Whitt Braddock's son and Jewell's sister together, making a baby.

The town, and his family, would have a field day with

it. That'd be minor, though, compared to the firestorm going on inside Aiden, but he pushed all those feelings aside for now. It was going to take every bit of his concentration to get them out of this alive.

Aiden had already called for backup. Not using normal channels in case these brainless wonders had indeed managed to plant bugs in his office and others. Instead he'd used his personal cell to phone his deputy Leland Hawks.

With any luck Leland would be here within twenty minutes.

That was way too long for Leland to help save Kendall and him, but Aiden had told the deputy to make a loud approach. Lots of sirens. Hopefully, the noise would send the guys on the run so that Aiden could track them down.

If this fight didn't end with the men's deaths, that is.

Aiden wanted one of them alive, though, if at all possible. Because when this was all said and done, he wanted answers as to who was really behind this.

Another shot smacked into the tree. Though it was hard to hold back, Aiden didn't return fire yet. He didn't have a lot of ammo and didn't want to waste any bullets in case this went on too long. But he did glance out at the pair to check on their latest position. They were in front of the SUV again. Where they were well protected.

Aiden couldn't say the same for Kendall and him.

The tree wasn't that wide, and he figured these two had brought enough firepower with them to tear right through the young oak. Added to that, there weren't any wider, thicker trees nearby for Kendall and him to move behind. Just plenty of underbrush and wildflowers, and none of that would stop bullets.

Kendall looked up at him, her eyes wide. Her breath gusting. Her body trembling. "Thank you for coming back for me."

That riled him. Of course he'd come back for her. It was his job, and there was no way he'd let something personal get in the way of the badge. She probably hadn't meant it as an insult, but it was.

"I found some scissors in the SUV, cut off the plastic cuffs, but then I got so dizzy," she added.

She was still terrified, just as she had been kneeling on the floor of his house. Aiden didn't want to know what kind of effect this was having on her unborn child.

It couldn't be good.

But it was better than the alternative. If those men had gotten Kendall away from his place, they would have killed her. Even if he'd done what they asked, that wouldn't have saved her life.

Then they would have come after him.

"You've lost some blood," he reminded her. "That's why you got dizzy."

No need to mention that it could be shock, but he hoped that wasn't the cause. He might need Kendall's help before this was over, and something like shock could incapacitate her.

"When the smaller one came at me, I stabbed him with the scissors," she said. "Twice."

She looked a little sick about that. Understandable. Most people were never in a position where they were forced to do bodily harm, but Aiden was thankful for the scissors and the stabbing.

"You did what you had to do," he let her know and then cursed himself for sounding so sympathetic.

He didn't want her to suffer. Not over some injury she'd managed to inflict on this homicidal idiot, but each kind word from him, each thought about this pregnancy nipped at barriers that had to stay in place when it came to Kendall.

"Leland's on the way," Aiden whispered when her trembling got worse. "That means we'll have backup soon, and we'll be okay."

Kendall nodded, and he figured she was trying to look a lot stronger than she felt right now.

Another bullet flew at them. Then another. And soon they were coming nonstop. Aiden had hoped it wouldn't come down to this, but the men were no doubt getting desperate, since they knew he probably had help on the way. That meant they had only two choices.

Escape or try to recover their hostage.

They appeared to be going for the latter, though the two had to know they could kill Kendall in the process. Of course, they could be doing cleanup.

Trying to eliminate *all* witnesses.

If so, these next few minutes were going to be bad, because Aiden had no intention of making an elimination easy for them. Nope. He was fighting back along with being fighting mad. How dare these morons pull a stunt like this in his own yard and house!

Now the problem was trying to figure out how to stop them from getting lucky with their elimination attempts.

Aiden knew every inch of his property, and there was a dry narrow gully about ten yards behind Kendall and him. Not as close as he would have liked, but maybe if he could distract these guys long enough, Kendall would be able to crawl to the gully, where she'd be better protected from the bullets.

"I didn't have any part in this," she said. Another look up at him.

Damn. He had enough uncomfortable things running through his mind right now without adding her emotions.

"Yeah. I figured that out." Too bad he had plenty of other things to figure out.

"And I meant what I said about leaving," Kendall added. "I had no intention of ever telling you about the baby."

The woman knew how to rile him. In the middle of a gunfight no less. Aiden didn't have a clue how he felt about this pregnancy, yet, but he darn sure hadn't wanted her to hide it from him. And Kendall had rattled that off as if he'd be pleased about her plan to sneak off.

Well, he wasn't.

Of course, right now he wasn't pleased about much of anything except that Kendall and he were still breathing.

Aiden glanced out at the two men again. They were still in place where he couldn't blow off any of their body parts. Then he glanced at Kendall.

But not at her face.

Too much emotion there for him to deal with, but he needed to see how her arm was holding up. The bleeding had stopped. That was something at least. But that gash was deep, and it had to be throbbing like a bad toothache.

"How does your arm feel?" Aiden asked, and he fired a shot at the men just so they wouldn't try to move closer.

"I'm okay."

A lie, for sure, but Aiden would take it for now. He'd already asked Leland to bring out an ambulance, but the medics wouldn't get close to the place with shots being fired. That was yet another reason for Aiden to put an end to this.

"I need you to get to the ground," Aiden said. "Stay behind me and stay down. Crawl to the gully." He tipped his head in that direction.

Kendall glanced over at the gully. Then at him. "But what about you?"

"I won't be far behind."

Possibly a lie as well, but Kendall had enough fear

running through her without his spelling out that there'd be no one to cover him if he tried to move from the tree to the gully. No, it was best for him to make his stand for as long as he could behind the tree.

She finally gave a shaky nod and inched herself lower to the ground. It wasn't easy. They were plastered against each other—her backside sliding against a part of him that needed no such touching. Especially from her. He got a split-second jolt of the blasted heat that'd always been there between them.

Thankfully, the fresh round of bullets slugged that heat aside.

He pushed Kendall all the way down until she was practically on her belly and then crouched by his side. "Move slowly if you have to." Because of her injured arm and the pregnancy. But Aiden was really hoping that she could do this fast.

Aiden leaned out, took aim at the front of the SUV and fired a shot just as Kendall started crawling.

She stayed down just as he'd ordered, and she moved through the wildflowers and other underbrush. Thankfully, fast. Still, Aiden fired another shot at the gunmen just to keep their attention on him. He breathed a little easier once he saw Kendall slide down and into the gully.

She was safe.

Well, maybe.

He'd parked just on the other side of the gully. Off the road and behind some trees. Aiden hadn't seen any other hired guns lurking around, but that didn't mean there couldn't have been some hiding.

The big talkative guy lifted his head, fired a couple of shots. Not the nonstop barrage like before. And in between the shots, Aiden heard the men talking. Or rather arguing.

Clearly, their plan had gone to Hades in a big ol' hand-basket by losing their hostage and what with one of them being on the business end of Kendall and her scissors. Now they were no doubt trying to figure out a way to salvage this, and it was possible the injured one needed some medical attention, too.

In the distance Aiden heard a welcome sound.

Sirens.

That got the men chattering even more, and Aiden braced himself for whatever they were going to try to throw at him next.

What they *threw* were bullets.

And lots of them.

The men fired into the tree. A volley of gunfire. All of it aimed at Aiden.

He ducked down, trying to shelter his body as best he could, but he was getting pelted with flying pieces of wood from the tree and other debris that the bullets were kicking up from the ground. There was no way he could lean out and try to get off a shot of his own. It'd be suicide, so he stayed put and prayed that he got a break soon.

He got it.

But it wasn't the break he had in mind. The shots slowed to a trickle, but even over the sound of the blasts, he heard another one.

The SUV.

One of them had started up the engine.

No. It was too soon for this to happen. Judging from the sirens, Leland was still a quarter of a mile out. Maybe more. These guys could get away before Leland even arrived.

Aiden moved to the other side of the tree, leaned out just a fraction and saw the two men already in the SUV. Only one, the injured one on the passenger's side, was firing through the open door, and even though his aim seemed wobbly, he still hit the dang tree.

Aiden had to dive back behind it for cover.

"Stay down!" Kendall yelled.

He wanted to curse when he saw her lift her head. "*You* stay down," Aiden snarled right back at her.

Aiden leaned out again. Took aim at the guy who was firing. And he pulled the trigger.

His bullet smacked right into the man's chest, and just like that, the guy tumbled out of the SUV and onto the ground. If he wasn't dead, he soon would be. But that wasn't Aiden's concern now.

It was the driver.

The chatterbox gunman hit the accelerator and flew out onto the gravel road that fronted Aiden's property. He fishtailed, the tires bobbling over the uneven surface, but that didn't slow him down nearly enough.

Aiden raced out from cover, bracketing his shooting wrist with his left hand, and he kicked the injured gunman's weapon aside. In the same motion, Aiden took aim at the SUV.

The bullet Aiden fired slammed into the back window, shattering the glass into a million little pieces.

But the driver kept going.

Aiden ran after him, took another shot. He missed. Then another. That one hit the SUV. At the right angle to have injured the driver, but Aiden couldn't be certain of that.

Because the SUV sped away.

Chapter Four

Kendall watched while the medic dabbed the wound on her arm with antiseptic and gave her a shot. The throbbing pain quickly turned to fire, but she clamped her teeth over her bottom lip so that Aiden wouldn't hear the groan bubbling up in her throat. He already had enough to handle without adding more concerns about her injury.

Not that Kendall expected him to be overly concerned about her, but at this point, anything and everything would feel like more weight on his shoulders.

The gunman who'd gotten away.

The dead one Aiden had been forced to kill in a shoot-out.

And then, of course, the bombshell about the pregnancy.

Aiden wasn't dealing with that—yet. He was still on the phone with his deputy who had a team out searching for the man who'd shot her. It was his fifth call since they'd arrived at the Clay Ridge Hospital. She suspected there'd be plenty more before the night was over.

"I'll just do a couple of stitches," the medic said to her while he numbed the area around the wound with another shot. "Then I'll get you to the tech for an ultrasound."

A few stiches didn't sound serious at all, but the second

thing he said captured both Aiden's and her attention. Until his gaze snapped to hers, Kendall hadn't even been sure Aiden was listening to what the medic was saying, but he issued a quick "I'll call you right back" to his deputy and stared at the medic.

"An ultrasound?" Aiden questioned. "Is something wrong?"

The medic shook his head and got busy doing the stitches. "It's just a precaution, something Dr. Kreppner ordered because of the trauma Miss O'Neal's been through."

Kendall's breath rushed out. The emotions, too, and she was no longer able to choke back that groan. Sweet heaven, there had indeed been trauma—both physically and mentally—and the baby could have been hurt.

Aiden shifted his attention from the medic to her, and even though she couldn't fight back the tears, Kendall had no trouble seeing the conflict going on inside him. There was concern in his eyes, and the muscles in his jaw had turned to iron. Maybe because of the possible danger to the baby. Maybe because of her tears.

Or perhaps both.

"Don't borrow trouble," Aiden said to her, his voice a low growl. "You heard what he told you, that it's just a precaution."

Kendall nodded, but she wouldn't breathe easier until she knew that all was well. She was only twelve weeks pregnant, and she wasn't even sure what an ultrasound could tell them exactly. Hopefully, it would be plenty enough to rid her of this overwhelming fear.

Her tears continued, clearly something that didn't please Aiden, because he huffed and handed her some tissues that he grabbed from the examining table.

"Thanks." She blotted her eyes and cheeks, looked up at him. "And for what it's worth, I'm sorry."

That apology covered a multitude of things, including his learning about the baby and this attack that could have gotten them all killed.

Her *I'm sorry* didn't cause his jaw to relax, though. "We'll talk about the baby later. For now, I want to know anything you haven't told me about what those men said to you. And no, I'm not accusing you of being a part of it. I just need to know anything that'll help us find that dirtbag who drove away in the SUV."

Kendall didn't especially want to relive the images of the attack or her kidnapping, but she also didn't want to focus on the pain that the stitches were causing in her arm.

"I don't know either of them," she started. "At least I don't think I do."

Aiden latched right on to that. "You don't *think* you do? Does that mean maybe there's something you recognized?"

"Maybe," she had to concede. "There was possibly something familiar about the one who did most of the talking, but I just don't know what. The other, however... the dead one...he had an accent. Jamaican, perhaps, and he was black, because I saw his hands." She paused. "I'm guessing he didn't have an ID on him?"

"Nothing, but we're running his prints now. Once we know who he is, we might be able to figure out who hired him." Aiden stared at her, apparently waiting for her to suggest who that might have been.

"I don't have a clue who hired them, but it wasn't me or any of Jewell's kids."

"You're sure?" he pressed.

She nodded. Prayed she was right about that. "Rosalie, Rayanne and Seth all love Jewell and want her cleared of the murder charges, but they wouldn't put me at risk to do that."

"They know about the baby?" he snapped.

Kendall shook her head. "Only your sister Laine knows. Like I said, she saw me coming out of the OB clinic. Since she'd also somehow heard rumors about us being together that night at the bar, she put one and one together."

"And she didn't tell me," Aiden grumbled under his breath.

"Don't blame Laine. I begged her not to tell you or anyone else." Much to her surprise, it appeared that Laine had kept her secret.

That comment earned her a glare from Aiden. "She's my sister, and she should have told me."

Kendall was about to ask if he had actually even wanted to know, but the medic eased a bandage on her arm and stood.

"What you heard in this room stays in this room," Aiden warned the medic. "Got that?"

Since Aiden could win an intimidation contest hands down, the guy was smart to nod. "Follow me to the ultrasound room."

As she probably didn't look too steady, Aiden took hold of her arm and helped her stand. Good thing, too, because the dizziness returned with a vengeance, and she had no choice but to lean against him. Judging from the way the muscles in his body stiffened, he wasn't pleased about that. Still, he hooked his arm around her and led her up the hall.

"You were just going to leave town," Aiden said, clearly not pleased about that, either. Of course, she hadn't said anything yet that'd pleased him.

Kendall nodded. "I thought it was for the best."

"Well, it wasn't." He probably said that a lot louder than he'd intended, because the medic glanced back at them. "I had a right to know that I made a baby with you that night," Aiden added in a much lower voice.

He said *that night* as if it were profanity. Which to him it probably had been. Kendall had felt the same way, too, immediately afterward. Yes, Aiden and she had skirted around this attraction for years, but with their families at serious odds, a one-night stand had been a stupid thing to do.

"I won't think of this baby as a mistake," she clarified.

She figured he would disagree with that, but he didn't. Kendall also figured he wouldn't go into the ultrasound room, but once they reached it, Aiden waltzed right in.

"I'm staying," he insisted before she could give him an out.

Again, the medic looked at them, his volleyed glances finally landing on Kendall. "The tech won't be long, but I can wait here if you want." There was concern in both his tone and expression. However, Kendall shook her head to assure him that it was all right for him to go.

"It'll be okay." Well, she'd be safe with Aiden at least, but Kendall could feel a mighty storm coming her way.

About the baby.

About her decision to leave him out of this.

"Okay, then." The medic tipped his head to her arm. "If you need something for the pain, just let the ultrasound tech know, and I'll have the doc write a script."

Kendall thanked him, knowing that she wouldn't be taking any painkillers even if she needed them. They'd be too risky for the baby.

The medic stepped out, finally, and Aiden didn't wait long to get that storm started. "How long have you known you were pregnant?" he asked.

"For about two months." She probably would have figured it out sooner if she hadn't been in complete denial. Denial about a possible pregnancy anyway. The memories of that night had stayed with her.

Big-time.

She'd lusted after Aiden for so many years. Too many. They were both thirty-six now, and the heated looks had started about twenty-three years earlier. The heat clearly had some staying power, because even drunken sex had fulfilled more than a fantasy or two. Sadly, Aiden had lived up to those fantasies in spades. If any part of it had been lacking, she maybe could have finally pushed Aiden out of her head.

So much for that happening now.

Especially since he was right in front of her. And his scowl and bunched-up forehead weren't the lust killers that they should have been. Probably because even with a scowl, Aiden managed to make most men look just plain ordinary.

"Jewell doesn't know?" he asked.

Kendall shook her head. "I figured I'd tell her after the trial."

That deepened his scowl. "A trial that might not happen if the goon in the ski mask gets his way."

She hadn't even thought of that. If whoever was behind this couldn't get Aiden to destroy the evidence, then he or she might just hire someone else to do the job.

"I've had the evidence moved," Aiden said. "It's being couriered to the Ranger Lab in Austin. So Jewell's out of luck when it comes to that."

Maybe out of luck, period. The bone fragments had been identified as belonging to Aiden's father, and that meant Jewell had means, motive and opportunity to have killed the man who was supposedly her lover. It certainly didn't help that Jewell wasn't denying the deed.

And now this.

If this was linked back to Jewell, the DA could tack on some obstruction of justice charges along with other assorted felonies like kidnapping and attempted murder of a county sheriff.

"Even you have to admit that it would be stupid for anyone connected to Jewell to try to destroy evidence," she said.

Aiden made a sound of agreement. "Stupid, yes, but that doesn't mean it didn't happen. I'll be looking at Jewell's daughters and stepson. Joplin, too."

Jewell's lawyer, Robert Joplin. Of all the suspects that Aiden had just listed, he was the one at the top of Kendall's list. Because Joplin was hopelessly in love with Jewell. Had been for years and would do anything to save her. However, that didn't mean Joplin was the only one with motive for this attempted fiasco.

"I hope you'll look at your own family, too," Kendall tossed out there. "Your mother and sister Shelby aren't exactly fans of Jewell, and they might have done something like this to make her look even more guilty."

And while that wasn't as strong of a motive as her family's, Jewell knew that Aiden's family had secrets.

Secrets that even Aiden might not know.

She braced herself for him to jump to their defense. Didn't happen. "I'll be talking to them and anyone else who hated Jewell and my father."

Good. But then, she'd figured all along that Aiden would be thorough. He was loyal to his family. Well, mostly. He didn't exactly have a friendly relationship with his mother, but Aiden would never forget that he was a Braddock.

Never.

Ditto for remembering that she was an O'Neal.

The door eased open, and Aiden automatically reached for his gun. After what'd happened with the gunmen, Kendall didn't blame him, but she was thankful it was a false alarm.

"I'm Becky Lovelle," the young blonde said. "I'll be doing your ultrasound."

Kendall certainly hadn't forgotten about the ultrasound, but her strained discussion with Aiden had pushed the reminder of a possible problem to the fringes of her thoughts. No fringes now, though. Her heart went into overdrive.

"This won't hurt," the woman said.

But Kendall was already tuning her out, her attention nailed to the screen. It was blank now, but soon she'd see her precious baby. Hopefully, unharmed.

Aiden didn't move closer. In fact, he leaned against the wall and watched from there. Even when the tech pushed up Kendall's top and shoved down her skirt to expose her belly and coat it with some goopy gel, he kept watching.

Kendall suddenly felt way too bare with Aiden in the room, but there was no way she'd convince him to leave. There was no way to convince Aiden of a lot of things, and once she had the all-clear with the ultrasound, she'd need to figure out a way to handle him and this situation.

Aiden wasn't going to like it when she insisted she leave.

But she would insist on it.

And maybe Aiden would soon see that it was the right thing for all of them.

The tech put the wand on Kendall's stomach, and when she moved it around, Kendall could see the baby's beating heart. Her breath rushed out.

"The baby's okay?" Kendall immediately asked.

"Appears to be. That's a strong, steady heartbeat." The woman continued to move the wand, and even though it was hard to make out some of the images, Kendall definitely spotted two arms and two legs. All moving.

"Amazing," Kendall said. "So much movement, and I haven't even felt it yet."

"Is that normal?" Aiden snapped.

The tech nodded. "Some women don't experience quickening or movement until week twenty."

That meshed with the maternity books that Kendall had been reading, but obviously this was all new to Aiden. He moved closer to the screen, his focus on the tiny baby.

Their baby.

Kendall saw and heard the moment that it finally sank in for him. Aiden made a hoarse sound that came from deep within his throat, and he mumbled something while his eyes tipped toward the ceiling. Maybe asking for divine help. She'd done that a few times early on, as well.

He dragged in a long breath. "Yeah, you should have told me."

That didn't sound like a man on the verge of rejecting fatherhood. Or even putting this in perspective. The bottom line was his family wasn't going to embrace this child, and hers likely wouldn't, either.

"Is that what I think it is?" Aiden asked.

Because he was looking gobsmacked again, Kendall's gaze rifled back to the monitor, and she tried to brace herself for whatever had put that bleached-out expression on Aiden's face.

"I'm sorry," the tech said, sending Kendall's heart into a tailspin again. "It's usually not that clear this early on, and I should have asked first if you wanted to know the sex of the baby. This is a new machine, and it gives much clearer images than we used to get with the old one."

Oh. Kendall got it then. Nothing was wrong with the baby, but the ultrasound had obviously shown her something she hadn't known before now.

The baby was a boy.

"A son," Aiden said, staggering back a bit.

Kendall had never seen him like this. Aiden was always in control. Always in charge. But this news had shaken him to the core.

"This doesn't change anything," Kendall insisted.

But she had the feeling he would have had the same reaction if it'd been a girl. It was just that seeing the baby on the screen made everything, well, real.

"The doctor will look over these images," the tech said, finishing up. She wiped the goop off Kendall's stomach. "But everything looks fine, right on target for the end of the first trimester."

The moment the woman stepped out of the room, Kendall fixed her clothes. Best not to feel exposed when she had this discussion with Aiden. A discussion he wasn't going to like. It was also a discussion she didn't even get to start because Aiden's phone buzzed, indicating that he had a text message.

"Leland got a hit on the dead guy's prints," Aiden said, reading the info on his phone. "His name was Montel Higgins."

She repeated it, hoping that it would jog some kind of memory. It didn't. "He has a record?"

Aiden nodded. "Both here and in his home country of Jamaica. He's worked as muscle for loan sharks but never anything this serious. Leland's checking to see if he can find a money trail so we can figure out who hired him."

Good. That was a start. "What about the other one? Any sign of him?"

"Not so far, but they'll keep looking."

Kendall didn't want them to stop looking, but she had to be realistic. It'd been several hours since the men kidnapped her, and the one who got away was probably long gone by now.

She stood, straightened her clothes. "You ready to talk?"

His gaze drifted to the ultrasound screen that was now blank. "Not about that. Not yet. But if you're up to it, I need to take your statement about the attack. You might be able to recall some detail that'll help us figure this out."

Kendall definitely wasn't feeling up to reliving the nightmare or giving a statement. She was exhausted and dizzy, and her arm was throbbing. Still, if she didn't do it now, she'd only have to go to Aiden's office tomorrow. Besides, she wasn't exactly looking forward to returning to her house right now. Not with that escaped gunman still at large.

Aiden got her moving out of the ultrasound room and into the hall, but he stopped when they reached the glass doors that led from the ER to the parking lot. He slid his hand over his gun and looked out, his gaze slashing from one side of the lot to the other. Since it was close to 9:00 p.m., there weren't many cars, only those of the workers and the handful of people in the ER itself. But Aiden still took his time, no doubt making sure they weren't about to be attacked.

"Wait here," he said. "I'll get my truck and bring it right to the door."

However, he didn't even make it a step before Kendall spotted movement in the parking lot. Aiden saw it, too, because he pushed her behind him and drew his gun.

But it wasn't the masked attacker coming back for another round.

It was a woman Kendall instantly recognized, and she groaned. It was almost as loud as the one Aiden made.

His mother, Carla, was making a beeline toward them.

Since Carla and she didn't live in the same town and definitely didn't travel in the same circles, it'd been a decade or longer since Kendall had seen the woman. She hadn't changed a bit. Tall and lean and dressed to perfection in a spring-yellow dress. Her dark blond hair was swept up and her makeup flawless. She looked ready for a church social.

Except for that troubled expression.

Aiden grumbled something Kendall didn't catch and maneuvered her back, away from the door.

"Your deputy said you were here," Carla greeted.

"I'm fine. I wasn't hurt."

"Good to hear." She spared him a glance as if it was the last thing she'd intended to ask about. And it probably was, since her attention stayed on her son for only several brief moments before it went to Kendall.

That definitely wasn't a loving look she gave Kendall.

"I figured I'd find you here with my son," Carla complained.

Aiden tapped the badge clipped to his belt. "She's with me because I'm doing my job. Two men kidnapped Kendall, and she was shot."

Again, that didn't appear to be what Carla had come to discuss. "Kendall O'Neal's not only a job to you." Carla's breath shuddered, and tears watered her eyes. "How could you crush me like this, Aiden? How could you let Jewell McKinnon's sister seduce you?"

Oh, no. Not this. Not now.

"It wasn't like that," Aiden insisted, but he might as

well have been talking to the air, because his mother didn't even look at him. She was glaring at Kendall.

"I know what happened between Aiden and you," Carla said to Kendall. "And now we need to figure out what we're going to do about this baby you're carrying."

Chapter Five

Aiden really didn't need his mother in his face right now. His fun meter was at zero, and judging from the start to this particular conversation, everything about it was going to fall into the nonfun category.

He could go two ways with this. Placate Carla with some kind of "we'll discuss this later" and go ahead and take Kendall to his office to get started on the paperwork. Or he could confront his mother as to how she'd learned about a one-night stand that Aiden hadn't mentioned to a soul.

Since he figured the first option had little chance of ending this conversation in a hurry, he went with the second route and maneuvered them to the corner of the room so they could have a semiprivate talk.

"Did Laine tell you?" Kendall asked.

Aiden got his answer to that when Carla's eyes widened. Those eyes then slashed toward Aiden. "You told Laine but not me?" But his mother waved off any answer that he might have given her. "It doesn't matter. Laine and I aren't on speaking terms since she married a McKinnon."

Yeah, and it was something his mom brought up often. Laine had indeed married Tucker McKinnon, Jewell's own son, and they were the parents of adopted twins. Something that had put a permanent rift between Carla and Laine.

Now Aiden was about to give her the same reason for a rift.

"If Laine didn't tell you, how did you find out?" Aiden asked. Not that it was critical for him to know how the proverbial cat had gotten out of the bag, but he wanted to know just who was feeding information about him to his mother.

"I'd rather not say," Carla insisted. "I'd rather focus on how to deal with this baby."

Kendall sighed. "My baby isn't something you need to *deal with*." Her voice was strained, and while her words were crisp, Aiden figured it was better than her telling Carla to mind her own business.

But his mother would see this baby as her business.

"You're wrong," Carla answered. "You're carrying a Braddock. My son's blood. And I can't let my grandbaby be raised by someone whose kin murdered my husband." She pointed to Kendall's stomach. "Your sister murdered that baby's own grandfather."

Oh, yeah. This was definitely not going in a fun direction.

"Someone shot Kendall," Aiden said in case his mother had already forgotten. "The doctor wants her to get some rest." The doc hadn't specifically said that, but Aiden figured rest was much preferred over another dose of stress that his mother was doling out. "You wouldn't want to do anything to cause her to miscarry, would you?"

Aiden hoped the answer to that was no, but his mother didn't budge.

"This won't take long," Carla insisted. Now her gaze came back to his. "Then you and I can have a private discussion tomorrow." The tears threatened again, followed by a whimper. "Why couldn't you just leave Kendall alone?"

Aiden had asked himself that a thousand times and still didn't have an answer. He'd developed an itch for Kendall about the same time he'd started to grow chest hair, and that itch had resulted in a kiss when they were thirteen. Kendall's first. There probably would have been more kisses in their immediate future if just days later they hadn't learned that his father had been murdered, and Kendall had left town with Jewell.

Of course, Kendall had come back to the area a time or two. Just enough to remind him that scratching the itch would feel pretty darn good even if it would also carry a huge price tag. Like now.

Except he didn't want to think of his baby as a *price tag*.

At the moment, he didn't want to think of his baby at all, because it wasn't a good idea for him to be focusing on something that could bring him to his knees when he had a would-be killer gunning for his head.

"You're just like your father," Carla added, giving Aiden another dig. "Unable to resist an O'Neal woman. At least he didn't get Jewell pregnant, though. Now we'll have a baby to raise."

Uh-oh. Definitely not the right thing to say, and Kendall stepped in front of him. "You're not raising my baby." She slid her hand protectively over her stomach. "In fact, you have no say in this whatsoever."

The little glance that Kendall shot him was probably to let him know that he didn't have a say, either. She was wrong about that.

Here came the tears, spilling down his mother's cheeks.

Since this was about to get uglier than it already was, Aiden took hold of Kendall and eased her back away from Carla. "Mom, I need to get Kendall's statement so I can figure out who tried to kill her and the baby."

That got Carla's attention. She'd obviously known about the attack, but it probably hadn't occurred to her yet that anything bad that happened to Kendall also happened to the baby she was carrying. Of course, maybe Carla didn't care about that at all, despite her insistence about raising the child.

"Any idea who kidnapped me and tried to force Aiden to destroy evidence?" Kendall demanded. And it was indeed a demand. There was plenty of anger in her voice and narrowed eyes when they landed on his mother.

"What evidence?" Carla questioned.

"The bone fragments," Aiden supplied.

Carla pressed her hand on her chest as if to steady her head. "Those fragments will convict Jewell of murder. There are only a handful of people who'd want that evidence destroyed. Joplin, Jewell's children and Kendall."

"And you," Kendall added.

Obviously, his mom hadn't seen that coming.

Neither had Aiden.

"You're under psychiatric care," Kendall added a heartbeat later. "Any other secrets you'd like to tell us about?"

Aiden was about to assure Kendall that it wasn't true, but his mother certainly didn't jump to deny it. "How did you know that?" Carla demanded.

Ah, heck.

Apparently, another can of worms had just been opened.

"I'd rather not say," Kendall answered, repeating the words his mother had said earlier.

That put some fire in Carla's eyes. "So what if it's true

that I'm seeing a psychiatrist? That doesn't mean I would try to have evidence destroyed."

"You might if you thought it'd make my sister look bad." Kendall paused. "Or if you thought it'd get rid of me and the Braddock baby I'm carrying."

Aiden mentally repeated his *ah, heck* because he didn't like the sudden look in his mother's eyes. The fire was still there, but he also saw something else.

The hatred.

It'd always been there, of course. But Aiden saw it now in a whole new light. Carla loathed Jewell, and that loathing extended to Kendall, since Jewell had practically raised Kendall after their father died.

Maybe his mother's hatred extended to the baby, too.

Yeah, Carla had demanded to raise the child, but he hoped like the devil that there wasn't something else going on here. Something that had caused her to put Kendall and the baby in danger.

But then he mentally shook his head.

There were plenty of other suspects with a more obvious motive without his reaching, and motive was something he'd take a hard look at soon. Right now he needed to fix this. Kendall was wobbling again, leaning against him, no doubt because she was dizzy. Probably in pain, too. No way did she need to be standing in the ER having words with his mother.

"We're leaving now. Come on," Aiden said to Kendall. "Mom, I'll call you."

And this time he didn't leave any room for argument. He got Kendall out of that corner and left his mother standing there, glaring at them.

Even though he was hurrying, Aiden didn't let his hasty departure make him stupid. He checked out the parking lot again to make sure no one was lurking around ready to attack.

There didn't appear to be.

Rather than leave Kendall there with his mother nearby, he drew his gun and hoped this wasn't a mistake.

"Hurry," he reminded her, though he figured Kendall wouldn't dawdle out in the open where her attacker could have another go at her.

Just in case that was the guy's plan, Aiden kept her close. Right against him to be exact. And even though he didn't break into a run, he got them to his truck as fast as possible. The moment they were inside and had on their seat belts, he drove away and got on the road that led out of town.

"I thought we were going to the sheriff's office," she said, glancing back at Main Street.

"It can wait. You have a security system at your house?"

She nodded but didn't look too certain about this decision. Heck, Aiden wasn't a hundred percent with it, either, but it might get Kendall the rest that she clearly needed.

He took out his phone, and while he kept watch around them, he called Leland. All his other deputies and Leland had their hands full with finding the missing attacker and processing the crime scene at Aiden's place, but Aiden needed some security measures for Kendall. That meant turning to someone he didn't especially want to turn to.

The McKinnons.

All three of Jewell's sons were lawmen. That was the good news. The bad news was they were estranged from their mother, since they blamed Jewell for leaving them after the affair with Aiden's father. An affair that'd led to his father's murder.

And that meant the McKinnon sons were also estranged from Kendall.

Still, he hoped the lawmen would do their jobs, since Kendall's house was in their jurisdiction.

"Call the Sweetwater Springs Sheriff's Office," Aiden told Leland when the deputy answered. "I'll need a protection detail out at Kendall's place."

She was already shaking her head before Aiden finished the request, and if Aiden could have thought of another way to keep her safe, he would have taken it. Leland assured him that he'd get right on that and then gave Aiden a quick update. When he was done, Aiden clicked the end call button so he could argue with Kendall. Not just about this but also the other surprise she'd dropped about his mother.

"Think about the baby," Aiden said. "Yeah, you and the McKinnon boys don't get along, but Cooper, Tucker and Colt will do their jobs. They don't have to like you to protect you."

He let that hang in the air.

"Obviously, that's true. You don't like me, and you're protecting me," she said.

Aiden thought about that a moment, and he decided there was no way to answer that so it wouldn't put him in butt-deep hot water. If he agreed that he didn't like her, it would only make this protective custody arrangement even more uncomfortable than it already was.

Besides, it was a lie.

He did like her. Well, her mouth anyway.

Okay, the rest of her, too.

He was just opposed to putting his mother and his sister Shelby through any more hell because of the choices that brainless part of him made in sleeping partners.

Of course, Kendall was more than just a former sleeping partner. She was the mother of his unborn son.

A reminder that required him to take a deep breath.

The fact they'd slept together didn't automatically mean he had to like her, but again reminding her that they were bad news for each other wouldn't fix anything right now.

"You'd rather I stayed with you than the McKinnons?" he asked, knowing the answer to that.

Now she was on the spot. Similar to him not liking her comment.

"It wouldn't be smart for you to stay with me," she answered.

Finally, they could agree on something, and once he had the McKinnon boys in place, he could get back to figuring out what the heck was going on and stopping any other attacks.

Not that he was positive there'd be another one.

The kidnappers had clearly lost, and with the evidence already moved, the danger might be long gone. Aiden hoped so anyway, but it still wasn't a risk he was willing to take.

He took the turn to Sweetwater Springs and moved onto the next subject. "How'd you know my mother was seeing a shrink? And spare me the answer of you'd rather not say, because that won't work with me."

"It worked when your mother used it so she wouldn't have to tell me how she found out I was pregnant."

"That ship hasn't sailed yet. I'll find out who told her. Now it's your turn to come clean."

She raked her fingers over her eyebrow and shifted in the seat a little. "I've been doing some checking, to try to find anything that might free Jewell."

Of course she had. "And you decided to check out my mother?"

Kendall nodded. "I had a PI follow her, and he reported back to me that she's been visiting a psychiatrist in San Antonio."

"My mother has a history of depression." Though he hadn't known about these visits to a shrink. Did that mean her depression had gotten worse? "It's a stretch, though, to think depression would have caused her to come after you to make Jewell look bad. Especially since I could have gotten hurt."

"But she knew about the baby," Kendall quickly pointed out. "Maybe she was willing to risk hurting you to make sure I'm out of your life for good."

It turned his stomach to think of that, and he wished he could totally dismiss it.

But he couldn't.

The truth was, his mother had been flirting with mental instability for years. All the way back to the time of his father's murder. He'd seen that vacant look in her eyes one time too many. Ditto for the sheer hatred that she just couldn't let go of. So yeah, news of a baby could have tipped her over the edge, and that was why Aiden needed to learn when she'd found out about the pregnancy and who'd been the one to tell her.

"While you were doing this checking and having people followed, did you hear anything else I should know?" he asked.

"Lee Palmer," she said without hesitation. "He also hired a PI to follow your mother."

Yet another hit of news that he hadn't been aware of.

Palmer.

The man's name kept turning up like a bad penny. A nearby rancher and his father's old nemesis. Palmer would love to see Jewell walk on this murder. Heck, Palmer would have loved to do the kill himself. Too bad he had a decent alibi for the time of Whitt's death. The man had been in the hospital recovering from a mild heart attack.

Still, Aiden had to shake his head on this one. "So, why would Palmer have my mother followed?"

"Maybe for the same reason I did." She paused. "He had your younger sister, Shelby, followed, too."

Aiden cursed. "And you didn't think you should come to me with this?"

Kendall lifted her shoulder. "You and I aren't exactly on the same side in this investigation, and technically I'm one of Jewell's attorneys. If anything had come up that was legally pertinent to the investigation, I would have disclosed it as I'm required to do. But a private citizen hiring a PI isn't something I have to disclose."

Hell's bells. She sounded like a lawyer and it set his teeth on edge again. "I'll have a talk with Palmer, and these little following adventures will stop." Aiden gave that some more thought. "Did he have me followed, too?"

"No, not that I know of anyway, but Palmer's digging into your old investigations. Into the McKinnon investigations, too. I think he's looking for anything that'll weaken the case against Jewell."

Yes, and he could try to smear Aiden's name in the process. He followed the law, but there was always a gray area or two when it came to investigations. Palmer better not be looking to throw him to the dogs to save the likes of Jewell.

Palmer also had better not be behind tonight's fiasco.

Apparently, Aiden had yet someone else to question, along with Jewell's attorney, Joplin. Maybe if he poked around enough, he'd find the snake responsible for that bullet Kendall had taken.

"I need some good news," she said, staring out the window into the darkness. "Any good news."

Aiden could possibly help with that. "Leland managed to get the surveillance footage from a camera just up the street from your office. One of the deputies is looking at it now to see if they can find any clues about the attack."

She shivered, rubbing her hands along the sides of her arms. Then she winced when her fingers brushed against the stitches.

Okay, maybe not good news for her after all. Because those images of being grabbed and dragged into an SUV probably didn't qualify as good. Still, if they didn't get anything from the dead gunman's past, then the footage was their best bet.

"How bad is your arm hurting?" he asked.

"It's manageable."

Which meant she was hurting. "I can call the doc and see if there's anything you can take."

But she shook her head. "You've already done enough."

That didn't exactly sound like a big thank-you, but Aiden let it slide. Soon, though, they'd have to talk about the final subject on his to-do list. The final and the biggest one.

The baby.

He took the turn into Sweetwater Springs. Since he'd never been to her place, Aiden followed her terse directions of "that way" and "here." He pulled to a stop in front of a house just one block off Main Street.

A whopping big house at that.

A reminder that Kendall was rich.

Her daddy, Travis, had been a rancher and plenty well-off. Travis had died when Kendall was just a kid, and the money, the ranch and all the other properties had been split between Jewell and her. Jewell had gotten the sprawling Sweetwater Ranch. Kendall, this house. Kendall's folks had divorced years before Travis's death, so her mom hadn't gotten anything, and then her mom, too, died the following year in a car accident, giving Kendall an even larger inheritance.

Aiden's family had money, too, but nothing like this.

"I don't have my remote to open the garage," she said. "The kidnappers took my purse, but I can use the keypad by the front door to unlock the house."

"No butler to let you in?" he mumbled, immediately hating the snark.

"He has the night off," she zinged back. A reminder of one of the things that had always attracted him to Kendall. She was nobody's doormat.

Not even his.

Aiden looked around before they got out, and as he'd done in the parking lot, he quickly got them moving. They reached the front door, where she used the keypad. He hadn't thought there'd be any more surprises tonight, but he got one when he stepped into the foyer. Yeah, it was a mansion all right.

And an empty one.

Kendall pressed in some numbers to disarm the security system and then immediately reset it once they were inside.

"I put everything in storage so I could get the house ready to sell," she said, following his gaze to the rooms off the foyer. Also empty.

"Because you were leaving. Leaving without telling me you were pregnant." And yes, he meant for that to be a zinger.

Unlike her previous gaze dodging, she didn't dodge this time. She met his gaze head-on.

"I'm thirty-six, and I figured even though this baby wasn't planned, it's a good time for me to start a family.

I didn't want to shove my dreams down your throat just because you were the one who got me pregnant."

Ouch. "You're calling me a sperm donor?"

"I'm giving you an out that you'll likely want when you get past the emotional punch of seeing that ultrasound." Kendall didn't give him a chance to challenge that. "Your mother and sister are never going to accept me, and I'm not letting them raise my baby."

He couldn't argue with the last part or the emotional punch, but he could darn sure take issue with the first. "I don't want an out."

But man, it thinned his breath to understand what that meant.

He'd be a father to this baby, no matter who objected. Even if he'd probably suck at it. He hadn't exactly had a good role model, since his father was a cheating, mean old bastard. However, he was a better man than Whitt had been.

He hoped.

Aiden might have convinced Kendall and himself of that if his phone hadn't rung. "Leland," he greeted his deputy when he answered.

"We got a problem, boss. The McKinnons are tied up with an armed robbery at a convenience store just off the interstate. There's a hostage."

Aiden groaned. Not only for the hostage but for what that meant. "Can anybody else do protection detail for Kendall?"

"I'm working on it, but I figure you need to stay there with her."

He didn't miss the slathering of doom and gloom in his deputy's voice. "Why? What happened?"

"There's been a spotting of the SUV that Kendall's attacker used to get away." Leland paused, added some profanity. "Someone's on the way to check it out, but the guy's in Sweetwater Springs." The deputy paused. "Aiden, he was seen less than a mile from Kendall's house."

Chapter Six

Aiden was in her bed again.

Well, in her *bedroom* anyway.

Something that Kendall had sworn would never happen. Of course, their one night together hadn't happened here but rather at the Sweetwater Springs Inn. Because the inn had been walking distance from the bar, and they'd both had too much to drink to drive.

Now he was here, sleeping on the floor next to her bed, because that masked kidnapper might try to come after her again. If most of her furniture hadn't already been put in storage, he might have opted for a guest room. There were six of them in the sprawling house, but since the only bed had been hers, he'd taken the floor.

A wise move.

With tensions running so high between them, the last place she needed Aiden was in bed with her. Even if her body thought that would have been a stellar idea. Of course, her body was always making the wrong call when it came to Aiden.

As it was nearly seven in the morning, Kendall eased out of bed, trying to keep her movements slow and quiet so she wouldn't wake him. However, she wasn't able to muffle the little sound of pain when she flexed her arm.

It hurt. And had done so for most of the night. Still, it was far better than it could have been. The kidnappers could have killed her.

Not exactly a sunshiny thought to start the day.

She'd worn cotton pj's to bed, but she also pulled on a robe before she stood. Since Aiden was right there on the floor, she stepped around him so she could head to the adjoining bathroom. Or at least that was the plan. But one look at him, and her feet automatically stopped moving.

Another wrong call that her body made, but that didn't prevent her from looking at him.

He was a sight all right. No pj's for him. He was still wearing his jeans but had stripped off his shirt, boots and holster, and the stripping had left her with an unobstructed view of his toned chest and abs.

He had a six-pack.

And the hot outlaw looks to go with it.

His dark blond hair was a little too long, but the tousled look suited him and went along with that desperado stubble. Ditto for his gray eyes. She couldn't see them now that he was sleeping, but the color seemed to change. They could be stormy dark or cool as mist depending on his mood.

Most of the time when he was looking at her, Kendall got the stormy version.

"Ogling me?" he asked, and she got a full dose of that gray when he opened his eyes.

"Trying not to step on you," Kendall corrected. And yes, ogling him in the process. She didn't wait around to see if he bought her answer. Kendall headed to the bathroom.

"Stay away from the windows," Aiden called out, something he'd reminded her of a lot since they arrived at her house.

She listened but did take a quick peek outside to make sure that goon wasn't in her yard. No sign of him. She had mixed emotions about that. Kendall wasn't eager to have him anywhere near her again, but if he had been out there, then maybe Aiden could have captured him.

Kendall hurried into the bathroom so she could take a quick shower. And put on some makeup. Fix her hair, too, only to remember that she hadn't brought a change of clothes in with her. That meant putting the robe back on so she could get to the closet in the bedroom. When it came to being around Aiden, the more clothes, the better.

Clearly, he thought so, too, because when she went back in, he was dressed, sitting on her bed and talking on his phone. No more ogling his chest, but sadly, her brain reminded her of how he'd looked lying on her floor. A flash of another memory, too, when Aiden had been naked and in bed with her.

That helped ease the throbbing in her arm, but it didn't help with other parts of her. Nor did the long look that Aiden gave her. His gaze—stormy gray, as expected—slid from her head to her toes, and then he jerked his attention away as if disgusted with himself.

She knew how he felt.

The last time he'd looked at her that way, they had landed in bed, and she'd gotten pregnant.

That brought on another set of images, this time from the ultrasound she'd gotten the night before. Kendall went into the massive closet and slid her hand over her stomach.

A boy.

For weeks she'd wondered about the baby's sex, and now she knew. Ironic that when she was a teenager, she'd fantasized about marrying Aiden and having his son, and here she was carrying that child.

Of course, in her clueless teenage fantasies, Aiden and

she had been perfectly happy. Kendall was still thrilled about the baby, but there wasn't much else that she could slap that happy label on.

She dressed. Not easily, since every little movement of her arm gave her a twinge of pain, and some gave her more than a twinge. But she managed to get on a pale pink dress and sandals. An outfit that Aiden would probably consider too prissy, but she'd already put on some baby weight around her stomach, and most of her other clothes were too tight.

"Anything new on the kidnapper?" she asked when she went back into the bedroom and saw that he'd finished his call.

"Nothing. But Leland had the Rangers do a bug sweep of the office, and it's clean. No listening devices. I also found out from Laine that she wasn't the one who told Carla about you being pregnant."

Good. It was a small thing, but Kendall was glad Laine hadn't gone back on her word to keep it secret. "Then who told Carla?"

"Still working on that." He tipped his head to her bandage. "How's your arm?"

"Fine."

Ah, she got the stormy eyes again. "How's your arm?" he repeated. "And I'll keep asking until I get a truthful answer."

Kendall huffed. "It hurts, and the stitches are pulling. Satisfied?"

"Satisfied that you're in pain? No. Satisfied that we've moved past the polite-answer stage? Then yes. Because I'm thinking we're going to need more than polite responses when we talk about the baby."

She swallowed hard. Kendall had been expecting and

dreading this conversation, of course, but she wasn't sure she was up to what would no doubt turn into a full-blown argument. An argument that would include why she'd planned to leave town and never tell him about their son.

Aiden stood from the bed and walked closer to her. With that holster slung low on his hips, he looked like a Wild West outlaw, ready to draw. "So, why were you at the Bluebonnet Bar three months ago?"

Of all the questions she figured he would ask, that wasn't one of them. Nor was it something Kendall wanted to discuss. "Does it matter?"

He lifted his shoulder. "I'm just wondering if you went there with the idea of finding a sperm donor so you could get pregnant."

She laughed, definitely not from humor but from the absurdity of his suggestion. "You're kidding, right?"

Another shoulder lift. "You said it yourself. You're thirty-six and want a family. Maybe that's why we ended up in bed."

Good grief. The man could irritate every bone in her body with just a few questions.

It was stupid, but she grabbed a handful of his shirt, yanked him closer and kissed him. It took Kendall less than a second to prove her point, because there was a flash fire of heat. She certainly felt it, and judging from the husky groan that Aiden made, he felt it, too. Her body wanted to continue proving the point, but this kind of fire-playing was dangerous.

Kendall stepped back, tried to gather her breath. "That's why we ended up in bed together. Aided and abetted by some Jack Daniel's, of course."

He made a sound of agreement and pursed his mouth a little. A gesture that caused her body to clench. And beg for another round with Aiden. Something it wasn't going to get.

"So, what got you started on the Jack Daniel's?" he pressed.

Kendall hoped the flat look she gave him let him know she wasn't happy about this subject, but like with the arm question, Aiden wouldn't let go until he was satisfied that he'd gotten the truth.

"I'd gone to the jail that day to talk with Jewell." Kendall pointed her index finger at him. "And so help me, you'd better not try to use any of what I'm about to say against her."

That got his attention. And he nodded, eventually.

Kendall gathered her thoughts, tried to put this in the best light. Impossible to do, though. "I asked Jewell to tell me what happened that day your father died. I wanted her to explain how her DNA got on the bedsheets in the cabin."

A cabin where the prosecution was going to say that Jewell and Whitt had carried out their secret affair. An affair that'd ended in violence because Whitt had told Jewell that it was over and that he was reconciling with his wife.

"And?" Aiden prompted when she didn't continue. "Did you think someone had planted her DNA?"

"I'd hoped. But Jewell said it got there because she'd been on the bed. With your father," she added in a mumble.

It'd crushed her to hear that. Jewell had been a mother to her. Someone she loved unconditionally, but Kendall had loved Jewell's husband, Roy, too, and her sister had admitted to what the town had buzzed about for twenty-three years.

That Jewell was sleeping with a married man. Because why else would Jewell have been on that bed?

"So then I came right out and asked Jewell if she'd killed Whitt," Kendall continued. "But she said that was best left for the jury."

Aiden stayed quiet a moment. "You were finally convinced your sister's a killer."

Kendall took her time answering, too. "No, but I think she could be covering for someone."

Roy, maybe. Heck, maybe even Carla if Jewell was somehow rationalizing that she owed the woman because she'd been sleeping with her husband.

"You won't use this against Jewell," Kendall insisted, then paused. "Why were you at the Bluebonnet that night?"

"Looking for the cure to a really bad day." Aiden edged back a little from her. "Topping the list, I'd killed a man in the line of duty."

Kendall had heard about it—a shooting was big news in a small town—but she'd been so focused on her own problems, she hadn't realized what Aiden was going through.

"Running into me at the bar didn't help cure your bad day," she added.

But Aiden didn't answer. He drew his gun and hurried to the windows at the front of the house. Kendall heard the car engine then, but when she went to see who it was, Aiden pulled her behind him.

Then he cursed.

"It's Mr. FBI himself," Aiden grumbled. "Seth Calder."

His arrival was both a blessing and a curse. Seth was Jewell's stepson and therefore Kendall's step-nephew. She loved him like a brother, since they'd practically been raised together, but she was so not in the mood to face yet another surly man today.

Aiden was more than enough.

Kendall headed out of the bedroom and toward the stairs, but as he'd done at the window, Aiden got in front of her. Seth rang the bell, and he didn't wait even a second before he rang it again. Then not even another second passed before he pounded on the door.

"Kendall?" Seth called out.

Yes, definitely surly. He'd no doubt heard about the shooting and probably wanted to know why she hadn't called him. She didn't think he'd buy that the kidnappers took her cell phone.

The pounding continued while Kendall disengaged the security system, and then Aiden threw open the door. And there Seth was. All six feet three inches of him. Imposing. Irritated.

Worried.

Cursing, Seth reached for her and pulled her into his arms. "How bad were you hurt?" he asked in a hoarse whisper.

"Not bad." She stepped back to show him the bandage. Thank goodness there was no pain meter on it, because it was throbbing again.

Seth looked into her eyes, no doubt trying to ferret out the truth, and then his cool blue eyes landed on Aiden again. "What the hell's he doing here?"

"My job," Aiden answered. "What the hell are *you* doing here?"

Since this sounded like the start of a testosterone contest, Kendall shut the door and quickly tried to diffuse it. "Aiden saved my life, and when Cooper and the others couldn't come over to stay with me, Aiden volunteered."

"Well, he can go, because I'm here now," Seth snapped.

Aiden's hands went on his hips. "I don't think that's your call, FBI Agent Calder." He said Seth's title as if it were some kind of scarlet letter. "This is my investigation, and I'm staying close to Kendall until I find out who kidnapped her and put that bullet in her arm."

That would have sounded good if Aiden hadn't added an accusing glare that he aimed right at Seth.

Seth got in his face. "If you're suggesting I had any part in that, then you're a dead man."

Aiden gave Seth the same hard look he'd gotten. "Can you vouch for your sisters, too?"

"Yes. Can you vouch for yours?" Seth fired back.

"Yeah."

"Even the one who's been hounding me?"

"Shelby," Aiden provided on a huff. "My kid sister takes her investigative reporter duties a little over the top. But she sure wouldn't destroy evidence needed to convict Jewell. Shelby's determined to make Jewell pay."

"Then who the devil did this to Kendall?" Seth demanded, tipping his head to the bandage.

"Somebody who wanted evidence destroyed," Aiden readily supplied. "Or else somebody who wanted to make it seem as if Jewell or her kin was into evidence tampering. I'm looking into all the suspects."

Kendall couldn't get a word in edgewise, as Seth just talked right over her.

"There'd better be someone with connections to your family on your suspect list," Seth insisted.

She instantly thought of the conversation they'd had with Carla. Plenty of venom there, maybe enough to want Kendall dead while also making Jewell look even guiltier. Plus, there were things in Carla's past that she was keeping secret from her family. Since Kendall now knew that secret, she probably shouldn't keep it from Aiden. But she wouldn't tell him now, not with Seth ready to latch on to anything he could throw in Aiden's face.

And vice versa.

"There is someone with connections to my family on that list," Aiden admitted. "Lee Palmer. He hated my father enough to want to see Jewell walk for killing him."

"Or maybe Palmer did the killing himself," Seth fired back.

Aiden mimicked the same noncommittal sound that Seth had made earlier. "Palmer had an alibi, remember. And while your stepmother's trial is out of my hands, the attack on Kendall is all mine. I'll find whoever's behind this, and his or her butt is going to jail."

She finally found her opening when they paused. "Once the kidnapper's caught," she added, "and an arrest is made, I'll be okay. There'll be no need for protective custody."

Kendall hoped that would reassure Seth. It didn't. He glanced at Aiden and her, and she could almost see him trying to work things out in that hard head of his.

Seth had known about her attraction to Aiden for years. Since they'd been fifteen, and he'd caught her doodling Aiden's name in her school binder. He hadn't exactly been pleased about that, since the gossip was still hot about Jewell having killed Aiden's father, but Seth had let it pass.

She was betting he wouldn't let it pass this time.

Maybe he sensed something between them. Like that stupid kiss that'd happened upstairs only minutes earlier.

Once the gaze shifting had stopped, Seth's narrowed eyes settled on her. "What exactly is going on here?" He didn't wait for an answer. "And does *he* have anything to do with the reason you're selling this place and leaving?"

Since it wasn't much of a secret any longer, Kendall decided to spill it fast. "I'm pregnant. Aiden is the baby's father."

It got so silent that she could hear her own breath. Her heartbeat, too, after Seth turned an arctic stare on Aiden.

"If you accuse me of taking advantage of her," Aiden grumbled, "you're a dead man."

Seth gave Aiden another long, hard look. One that would have caused most men to take a step back. Simply put, Seth didn't just look dangerous with his black hair and dark blue eyes; he *was* dangerous. Well, he could be when it came to protecting his own, and Seth considered her one of his own.

But Aiden was dangerous in his own right.

"Does he want you to leave town?" Seth asked her.

A million-dollar question, and Kendall didn't know the answer. Maybe Aiden didn't know the answer, either.

"It's my baby," Aiden said.

All right. That wasn't exactly an answer to anything, but it sounded like some kind of declaration of war. Maybe it was. Her quiet exit out of town was already a bust, but any exit now would involve Aiden.

Maybe Aiden demanding to be part of her life.

Although it would create an even bigger rift between their families.

Seth went closer to her, took hold of her hand. "Just say the word, and I'll stay here with you."

It was a generous offer, but he no doubt had work. Plus, he was still looking for anything that would clear Jewell's name despite the fact that her sister wasn't cooperating with any of their efforts.

Kendall shook her head. "I'll be okay."

She hoped. And she also hoped that being okay didn't put Aiden and her on another collision course that would lead them back to the bedroom.

Definitely no more proving-a-point kisses.

"Call me if you need anything," Seth added, giving her hand a gentle squeeze. He shot Aiden another glare before he left.

Kendall rearmed the security system and turned to Aiden to get an explanation as to what his *it's my baby* comment meant, but his phone rang again. She saw Leland's name pop up on the screen. Unlike with the other calls he'd gotten or made throughout the night, Aiden put this one on speaker and went to the sidelight window to watch Seth drive away.

"Jewell's lawyer is in your office, demanding to see you right now," Leland greeted.

Aiden mumbled some profanity. "Tell him I'll be there soon. I'm bringing in Kendall to take her statement about the kidnapping." He was about to hang up, but Leland spoke before he could.

"There's more," the deputy said, and judging from his tone, it wasn't going to be the good news that Kendall was hoping for. "There's been another sighting of the missing kidnapper and his SUV. It was captured on the new traffic camera just off the interstate."

"Please tell me the guy's not headed here," Aiden snapped.

"No, but trust me, boss, you're gonna want to see this."

Chapter Seven

Aiden didn't like this latest turn of events with the missing kidnapper. The idiot had gotten much too close to Kendall again and had gone to a place that only made this mess worse: to the home of one of their suspects.

Lee Palmer.

There wasn't much about the past twenty-four hours that Aiden liked, but the kidnapper's mere presence at Palmer's meant there was a connection that could lead to Palmer's arrest. If Aiden could prove it, that is. He needed to find this kidnapper and get the investigation over and done with so he could settle some personal things with Kendall.

Well, settle one thing with her anyway.

The baby.

Aiden wasn't sure exactly what Kendall was expecting or not expecting him to do, but there was no way he was going to let her leave without some kind of guarantee that he would be part of his son's life.

His son.

And because that was still a little mind-numbing, Aiden pushed it aside so he could deal with the man who had demanded to see Aiden at the sheriff's office.

Robert Joplin.

Joplin was pain in the rear number one. The second pain in the rear was on the way there to Aiden's office, as well. Or at least he darn well better be, since Leland had ordered him to come in.

Palmer himself.

Talking to his dad's old foe wasn't pleasant on any day, but on this particular one, Aiden would have to ask the man some hard questions. It wouldn't be pretty, but if what the camera footage showed was true, then that idiot who'd shot Kendall had driven the SUV directly to Palmer's ranch.

Trust me, boss, you're gonna want to see this, Leland had said to Aiden when he called earlier. Leland had been right. Those images were something that could blow this case right open.

Aiden had another look at that footage that Leland had loaded on the computer in the squad room. Footage taken from a camera that'd been designed to monitor traffic on the interstate. He took his time, examining it frame by frame, despite the fact that Joplin was hollering for him to hurry up so they could talk.

Kendall watched the traffic footage, too, and she pulled in her breath when the SUV took the turn to Palmer's place. It was a grainy image but clear enough to see the license plate. Yes, it was the kidnapper all right.

So, why was he headed there?

And since Palmer's ranch was the only place on that entire road, then the man couldn't claim the hired gun was just paying a visit to someone else.

"Derek and Sarah are heading out to Palmer's place now to see if the SUV's still there," Leland explained.

Derek was the most experienced deputy that Aiden had, and he was glad the night-shift deputy, Sarah, was going with him for backup. Though maybe it wouldn't be needed, and the kidnapper would surrender peacefully.

Aiden could dream anyway.

"Does Palmer know about this footage?" Kendall asked.

Leland shook his head. "I thought it was best not to hear it over the phone. But I did tell him he should probably bring his lawyer."

Which Palmer would do. Since he was always operating just above the law, Palmer kept a team of attorneys to make sure he stayed out of legal hot water.

Leland glanced at the clock on the wall. Nine-thirty. "Palmer should be here soon."

That was Aiden's cue to get moving, and he turned to Kendall. "You want to get started on your statement while I talk to Joplin?"

She gave him a flat look. "Do you really think Joplin is going to leave without seeing me?"

He knew the answer to that—no. Since Kendall had worked with Joplin on Jewell's legal defense, they were allies. Aiden had just wanted to spare Kendall what would no doubt be another confrontation. Not with her. But Joplin sure wouldn't have any nice things to say to Aiden. He never did.

"After you talk with him and give your statement, I'll work on getting you a real protection detail," Aiden said.

"Maybe it won't be necessary if Palmer confesses to everything."

Aiden figured pigs had a better chance of flying before that happened. She'd need protection all right, and she would want anyone but him to guard her. Of course, that wouldn't stop him from doing it, but he did want plenty of backup. That meant a protection detail.

With Kendall right by his side, Aiden went to his office, and the moment they stepped inside, Joplin jumped to his feet and hurried to her. Much as Seth had done earlier, he took her hand.

"Are you all right?" Joplin asked, not waiting for an answer. "I tried to call, but it went straight to voice mail."

"The kidnappers took her phone," Aiden provided. And they'd obviously taken out the tracking device on it, since the Rangers hadn't been able to get a ping on it to find the location.

Joplin didn't even spare Aiden a glance or acknowledge the information. "I tried your home phone, too, and it's been disconnected."

"Because I'm moving." Kendall pulled her hand from his.

"Moving?" Joplin howled. "Why? Because of the attack?"

She shook her head. "Personal reasons."

Joplin's gaze turned to a glare, aimed at Aiden. "You're running her out of town."

Because Seth had already suggested pretty much the same thing, Aiden scowled at the lawyer. "I'm not running anybody out of town, but I do want you to tell me if you know anything about the attack."

Now, that caused Joplin to scowl. Aiden wasn't making many friends today. Not that he wanted Joplin for a friend.

"We just need to find out why those men wanted the bone evidence destroyed," Kendall said, and her tone was a lot nicer than Aiden's. Joplin seemed to respond to that, because his expression softened when he turned to her.

"I don't know." Joplin added a sigh and a head shake. "I talked to Jewell about it this morning, and she's appalled that someone would do this on her behalf. Or appear to do it on her behalf," he tacked on when he looked at Aiden.

"A Braddock's behind this," Joplin insisted.

"And which Braddock would that be?" Aiden asked, none too friendly, either.

"Your sister Shelby, maybe. Perhaps your mother."

That was another of those accusations that Aiden didn't want tossed around. "Nobody in my family wants those bone fragments destroyed, especially not as some kind of reverse psychology to suggest that Jewell is innocent. Because she's not."

But the moment he said that, Aiden got a thought. A bad one. The first he'd had of the sort.

What if Jewell truly was innocent?

Ah, hell.

This was about the kiss in Kendall's bedroom. And the baby. He was softening, and it wasn't a good time for that, since he didn't want the baby or a kiss to deter him from doing his job. Because the job might be the only thing that kept Kendall and the baby safe.

"Did you know the kidnappers?" Joplin asked her.

"No." She glanced at Aiden, who finished for her.

"But we have an identity on the one I killed. Montel Higgins. Ring any bells?" Aiden watched Joplin's face, looking for any kind of reaction.

However, he didn't get one. "No. Should it?"

Well, it would if Joplin had been the one to hire him. "We're checking now to see if he has any connection to our suspects."

Joplin didn't ask if he was a suspect, probably because he knew that he automatically was. Instead he turned back to Kendall. "I heard there were two attackers. Did you know the other one, maybe recognize his voice?"

"Aiden's already asked me that, and the answer's no. At least, I didn't recognize anything specific," she added in a mumble.

"Too bad," Joplin answered. Some emotion went through the man's eyes, and Aiden hoped it wasn't relief.

"Maybe you're behind the attack," Aiden said to Joplin, and he ignored the man's howl of protest and continued. "You're in love with Jewell. Everybody in town knows that, so maybe you made a really bad decision to use Kendall to destroy the bone fragments."

Joplin shook his head. "I didn't."

But then something happened. Joplin's gaze drifted from Aiden to Kendall's stomach. It was just a glimpse, but when Aiden's eyes met his again, it was clear that the lawyer knew something he shouldn't know.

That Kendall was pregnant.

Hell's bells. Did everyone in town know? And if so, how?

Better yet, how had the kidnappers found out? Because they'd certainly known that the baby would be the ultimate bargaining tool to get him to cooperate.

"Who told you?" Aiden came right out and asked Joplin.

Obviously, Kendall hadn't missed the look, either, because she stared at Joplin, waiting for him to answer.

"Carla," Joplin finally said.

That wasn't the answer Aiden had expected. "My mother told you?" he said with a whole boatload of skepticism.

"Carla called me yesterday morning out of the blue," Joplin continued with a nod. "She wanted me to confirm that the baby was indeed a Braddock. I told her I didn't have a clue, that I didn't even know Kendall was pregnant."

Yesterday morning. That would have been enough time for Joplin to throw together a kidnapping scheme so he could get the evidence destroyed. Of course, it would also be enough time for Aiden's mother to do the same. A plan to make the McKinnons or the O'Neals look guilty of obstructing justice.

If Aiden wanted to believe Carla could do something like this, he could buy it happening. But he wasn't ready to believe that just yet.

He hoped there wouldn't be any kind of proof to make him believe it, either.

"Did you tell Jewell about the baby?" Kendall asked, and yes, there was some concern in her voice now.

Joplin dodged her gaze. Not a good sign.

"I didn't tell her, but she guessed," Joplin explained.

Kendall threw her hands up in the air and then winced, no doubt because the motion pulled her stitches. "How?"

Joplin made an *isn't it obvious?* sound. "Jewell started speculating as to why kidnappers would have taken you and not one of Aiden's sisters. You and Aiden have always had a thing for each other, so it wasn't hard for her to figure it out."

A thing? Well, it was a stupid label for this unwanted attraction between Kendall and him. More like an Achilles' heel.

Kendall groaned. "I need to talk to my sister. *In person*," she added to Aiden, knowing that he would suggest a phone call instead of a visit.

Yes. But the timing sucked. "After you're done with your statement, I'll arrange to have you escorted to the jail." Or course, he'd be one of those escorts. He was dead serious about not letting her out of his sight until all this was cleared up.

"And then maybe you'll come stay with me," Joplin said to her.

Both Aiden and Kendall looked at him as if he'd sprouted hooves.

"You can't trust a Braddock," the lawyer added.

"But she can trust you?" Aiden fired back. "A man who'd do anything, and I mean anything, to get your old flame out of jail?"

Joplin certainly didn't deny it. "Jewell's innocent. That's the reason I'd do anything to set her free." And with that declaration he'd made too many times to count, Joplin picked up his briefcase, his attention still on Kendall. "At least consider my offer to stay with me. If not for your own sake, then for the baby's."

Aiden was already operating on a short fuse, and that did it. "Nobody will put as much into protecting the baby as I will, because it's my son."

Judging from the way the whole building suddenly got quiet, everyone inside had just learned that it was his son, too. Not that Aiden had plans to keep it from everyone. But he probably should give his sisters a call so they'd hear the news from him personally. Laine already knew and might not care to hear it repeated. She might not even talk to him, because she was now a McKinnon, and not a Jewell-loving McKinnon, either, since Laine was married to one of Jewell's estranged sons.

But Shelby was a different matter.

Shelby would see this as a slap to her and the family. A betrayal even. She darn sure wouldn't see her brother's attraction to Kendall as a *thing*.

Joplin smiled, likely pleased that he'd fueled Aiden's outburst. Or maybe he was just smiling because he was walking away scot-free after orchestrating an attack on Kendall. But if the man was guilty, he wouldn't be on the streets for long. Aiden would see to that.

"Sorry," Aiden said to her after Joplin left.

Kendall waved him off. "The pregnancy apparently

wasn't much of a secret anyway. Though I'd like to know who told your mother."

So would he, and Aiden took out his phone to do something about getting that info. However, he didn't even get to press his mother's number before he heard yet another voice.

Pain in the butt number two had arrived.

"Where is he?" Palmer's booming voice echoed through the building.

By *he*, Palmer no doubt meant Aiden, so he stepped into the hall. It was Palmer all right, dressed in his starched jeans, white shirt, bolo tie and cream-colored Stetson. Which he didn't remove. Aiden had never seen the man without it, and it was nearly the same color as his hair.

Palmer was in his early sixties now. The same age Aiden's dad would have been if he'd lived. Probably would have had the same build, too, with Palmer's middle going soft and paunchy. Still, Palmer managed to look strong and imposing, rather than a man who was nearly at retirement age.

As Aiden had predicted, Palmer had two lawyers with him. Both dressed in suits, both sporting nervy little expressions that reminded Aiden of twitching rats.

"Go ahead and let Leland take your statement," Aiden said to Kendall. "I'll handle this."

Did she listen?

No, of course not.

Kendall went straight to the computer on Leland's desk and pointed to the screen. "Did you send that goon after me?"

"Well, hello to you, too, Kendall. Long time no see." Palmer gave her a lazy smile that might have been genuine. From all accounts, he actually liked Kendall. Or maybe he just liked the fact that she was butting heads, legally speaking, with the Braddocks.

Kendall certainly didn't smile. "Did you hire two men to kidnap me and try to force Aiden to destroy evidence in my sister's case?"

As if he had all the time in the world, Palmer looked at the screen. At the image of the SUV taking the turn toward his property. If he was concerned one bit about what Kendall was asking, he didn't show it. Instead he smiled at Joplin when the lawyer joined them.

"Aiden's on a witch hunt," Joplin warned Palmer. "Beware."

Kendall shot Joplin a glance that could have frozen the desert a couple of times over. "The man in that SUV tried to kill us."

Her terse glance and comment caused Joplin to step back. "I should be going. I am free to go, right?" he asked Aiden. "Or do you plan to arrest me for something?"

"No plans, yet," Aiden snarled. "But it's early. Give me a few hours, and I'll see what I can come up with."

Joplin got his snarky look back and stormed out. Good. One pain down. Another to go. But Aiden wanted some answers from this one first before he went anywhere.

"Why don't we take this into the interview room," Aiden said to Palmer and his lawyers. Not really a suggestion. He hiked his thumb toward the hall and got them moving in that direction.

Aiden would have preferred that Kendall skip this, and he tried to let her know that with a raised eyebrow, but she just raised one of her own.

"You're just not gonna let go of this bad blood between us, are you?" Palmer grumbled as they filed into the interview room. "That feud with your daddy was a long time ago."

Yeah, it was. In fact, it'd happened twenty-five or so years ago when Palmer basically stole some Braddock land by falsifying old records. Something Aiden had never been able to prove, but he was certain that it'd happened.

"No, I wasn't planning on letting go of it," Aiden grumbled back. "I kind of like hanging on to bad blood."

Kendall's gaze came to his, and Aiden wanted to kick himself. Later, he'd have to let her know that their bad blood was going to have to get a whole lot better because of the baby.

Maybe that was possible.

Maybe.

"Bad blood aside," Aiden said, his attention back on Palmer now, "I'm more interested in why that hired gun in the SUV paid you a visit."

"He didn't visit me." Palmer didn't hesitate. "I wasn't at my ranch last night or this morning."

One of the lawyers extracted a piece of paper from his briefcase. "That's a receipt for Mr. Palmer's hotel room. He stayed in San Antonio on the Riverwalk last night and just got back. We came straight here."

Aiden figured Palmer would try something like this. That bad blood and Palmer's previous scummy dealings always made Aiden think the worst. Including that receipt.

"You got a guilty conscience or something?" Aiden asked the man. "Is that why you brought a receipt with you?"

Palmer shrugged. "I figured if you were calling me in, I'd need an alibi."

"That's not an alibi," Aiden informed him. Best to go with the direct approach and repeat Kendall's question. "It just means you possibly weren't at your ranch when the traffic camera recorded this. Did you hire that guy in the SUV to destroy evidence and then kill Kendall and me?"

Palmer's eyes widened, just slightly and for only a fraction of a second. "Are you okay?" he asked Kendall.

"No," she snapped. "Did you hear that part about somebody trying to kill us? Well, it was the man in the SUV that was on the road leading to your ranch."

Palmer glanced at the other lawyer, and the guy quickly took out a phone. To call the ranch, Aiden realized, because he asked to speak to Leonard Graves, one of Palmer's top dogs who was an overseer at the ranch.

"Did Mr. Palmer get any visitor in a black SUV?" the lawyer asked. A moment later, he ended the call and shook his head. "No visitors."

Maybe Graves was telling the truth, maybe not. Aiden's deputies should already be out at the ranch by now so they could have a look for themselves.

"There are plenty of ranch trails on my property," Palmer reminded Aiden. "As you well know, since you used to play out there as a kid."

Ah, a dig about the land deal. That always seemed to come up. But Palmer was right about the ranch trails. There were plenty of them, and they coiled all around his property.

"That doesn't explain why the kidnapper would go there," Aiden pointed out.

"Maybe because he wanted to make me look guilty." Palmer didn't hesitate.

Again, Aiden couldn't argue with what he was saying.

"Think about it," Palmer continued. "Whoever hired that nut job must have known about the traffic camera. Must have known that it would show the SUV turning onto the road that led to my land. If I'd hired him, then the last place I would have told him to come was my ranch."

"Unless the guy panicked when his partner was shot," Aiden supplied. "Or maybe he was hurt, too. I fired into the SUV, and I might have hit him. Maybe the guy needed a doctor and didn't have any other place to go but to the man who hired him."

That got a rise out of Palmer. His jaw locked. His eyes narrowed. "And I suppose you'll say I wanted him to force you to destroy some evidence to clear Jewell's name?"

"Well, it did cross my mind. Did you?"

Palmer huffed, shook his head. "What evidence?"

"The bone fragments." As he'd done with Joplin, Aiden watched for a response.

He got one.

The corner of Palmer's mouth kicked up into a smile. "Well, I gotta say if I was into evidence tampering, that's the lot I'd like to see destroyed. Without those bone fragments, the jury might not believe a man was even killed. And with Jewell's pretty face and angelic eyes, they might be inclined to let her walk."

In your dreams, Aiden nearly snapped, but then he remembered Kendall was right there next to him.

"If my sister is cleared of these charges," Kendall said, staring at Palmer, "it won't be because of her looks. It'll be because a jury will be convinced that she's not capable of murder."

"We're all capable, sweetheart," Palmer answered, and the *sweetheart* actually sounded like a term of endearment rather than sarcasm. "But I'm betting nobody in the county will want your sister to go to jail for ending the life of a miserable piece of cow dung like Whitt Braddock."

Now, here was the point where most sons would have taken exception to their daddy being called cow dung. But the truth was, Whitt just wasn't a good man. Not a good father, either. Well, not to Laine and him anyway. Shelby had barely been seven when their father was killed, and while he was alive, he'd always treated her like a princess.

That was the reason Shelby was fighting tooth and nail to see Jewell convicted. Aiden was just in it for justice.

Any old justice.

So that he could finally put this behind him.

Maybe then his mother would get her head back on straight, and Laine and he would have some peace.

But justice still wasn't going to change the fact that Palmer was right about this. Plenty of people wanted Whitt dead, and those same people didn't want Jewell punished for doing it. That included somebody who might hire kidnappers and send one out to Palmer's place just to make him look guilty.

Aiden silently cursed, because with that hotel receipt, it meant he didn't have any hard evidence to suggest that Palmer had even caught a glimpse of the idiot in the SUV, much less had contact with him.

Palmer knew that, too, because he stood, the lawyer duo standing at the same time. "If there's anything else, Aiden, just give me a holler."

However, before they could make it to the door, it opened, and Leland stuck his head inside. The deputy lifted a pair of handcuffs and looked at Aiden.

"We got it, boss," Leland said. "We got something we can use to make an arrest." His attention went to their visitor. "Lee Palmer, you have the right to remain silent..."

Chapter Eight

Kendall watched as Leland led Palmer away toward the holding cell. Palmer cooperated, all the while barking out orders for his lawyers to find a judge who'd get him out of there ASAP.

And with Palmer's money and connections, that would probably happen.

However, the evidence against him was pretty clear. First, the SUV driver going out to his ranch. Then the money trail Leland had found that linked a payment from one of Palmer's accounts to the dead kidnapper, Montel Higgins. Strong evidence but still maybe not enough to keep Palmer behind bars.

"I got a bad feeling about this," Aiden said.

So did Kendall.

It seemed, well, too obvious.

Palmer was shady, no doubts about that, but he wasn't stupid. Sure, he wanted Jewell to go free, but if he was truly behind this, why wouldn't he have better hidden his tracks? And Palmer definitely had the money to do that. He could simply have paid the kidnappers in cash, and there would have been no record of it.

"Maybe this is another case of reverse psychology?" Kendall suggested. Yes, she was reaching, but something wasn't right.

Aiden shrugged. "Or maybe one of Palmer's lackeys put this idiotic plan together and forgot to tie up a loose end or two."

Maybe. If so, then perhaps Palmer would call off any other "surprises" he might have planned to get Jewell released.

"Now, about that statement," Aiden added after a long breath.

She shook her head. "I need to see Jewell. I want to explain to her in person about the baby."

"Oh, I think she's already figured it out." But then Aiden huffed. "All right. I'll take you to the county jail, and after that you can do the statement, eat and then rest."

Kendall shouldn't have minded that Aiden gave the same importance to eat and rest as he did a mandatory statement about the kidnapping. It smacked of concern not for her exactly but for her condition. A red flag that Aiden was over his initial shock about the pregnancy and was now on to making plans.

Plans that would no doubt clash with the ones she'd already made.

Of course, she'd made those plans when Aiden didn't know about the baby, when she thought it would be best if she just left him out of things. But there was no way he'd be left out of it.

And that meant she needed to figure out what to do.

Aiden didn't say anything else until Leland had locked up Palmer in the holding cell. The lawyers hurried out of the building as if their tails were on fire, but they were probably just in a rush to find a judge or the DA, with the hopes of swaying one of them to let their boss out.

"Jeb, I need you to follow Miss O'Neal and me to the jail," Aiden said, motioning to the deputy in the corner. The young man practically jumped to attention.

Kendall didn't personally know him, but he looked barely old enough to be wearing a badge. Still, Aiden's pickings were slim, as his other deputies were tied up at Palmer's, and Leland had to man the office.

"This shouldn't take long," Aiden said to Leland.

As Aiden had done earlier before they started the drive to the sheriff's office, he looked out the window, no doubt making sure no one was waiting there. Once he opened the door, he hurried her to his truck. The drive was short, only about five miles and just outside town, but Jeb stayed right behind in a patrol vehicle.

"I'll be with you when you talk to Jewell," Aiden said out of the blue.

"No need. She'll probably be upset."

His glance was more of an *I beg to differ* look. "Sure, Jewell will be upset, and that's why I'll be there. We got in that hotel bed together, and there's no need for you to catch the flak for it on your own."

Kendall opened her mouth to argue that she didn't need Aiden as a crutch, but the truth was, she sort of did. Her nerves were raw, right near the surface, and the scrambled eggs and toast she'd had for breakfast were no longer feeling so great in her stomach. Another argument with Aiden wouldn't help, and besides, Jewell would probably want to see him anyway.

Not to yell at him, though.

Jewell wasn't the yelling type. But there'd likely be plenty of hurt in her eyes when she learned that her little sister had slept with the man trying to convict her of murder.

Aiden parked in his reserved spot right next to the county jail, and he gave his deputy a signal indicating that it was okay for him to return to the office, where Kendall was sure Leland would need some help processing Palmer.

The county jail wasn't a modern facility but rather a converted mental hospital that'd been built back in the 1920s. However, the rough limestone facade was definitely prison gray, and there were coils of razor wire ribboning around the top of the high metal fence.

Even though Aiden was the county sheriff, his deputies didn't staff the jail. The guards and warden were civilians, contracted and paid by the county. Still, Aiden's badge got Kendall and him in quickly through the two sets of security doors.

"We don't have an appointment," Aiden said to the guard at the final checkpoint. As part of protocol, Aiden handed the guard his primary and backup weapons, since only the guards were allowed to be armed beyond this point. "But we need to speak with Jewell McKinnon."

The bulky bald guy grumbled something about that not being a problem and motioned for them to follow him. "I'll get her for you."

The guard then put them in the visitors' room to wait while he brought Jewell out to them. Of course, they'd have to talk to her through the thick Plexiglas panel, but at least they'd be face-to-face.

"I hate that Jewell's here," Kendall said under her breath.

She hadn't exactly planned to say that aloud, but it was something Kendall felt every time she'd visited her sister over the past six months. Everything about the place was depressing from its concrete walls, its gray floors and the lingering smell of disinfectant and sweat.

"The trial's in less than two months," Aiden reminded her.

But that might only be the start of more jail time. And if Jewell was convicted of murder, she'd be moved to a prison much farther away.

They sat in the seats in front of the Plexiglas, but Aiden turned to her. "So, what will you say to your sister when she asks what we're going to do about the baby?"

Twenty-four hours ago, the answer would have been easy. She was leaving town to start a new life. But now her plans would likely have to be amended.

"I still think my leaving is a good idea. For your family's sake," she added when she felt his arm tense beside her.

"Your house in Sweetwater Springs is twenty minutes from Clay Ridge," he reminded her.

Yes, but her law office was in Clay Ridge, where she might run into a Braddock or two. Of course, she'd run into Aiden no matter where she ended up.

"How big a part do you think you want in this baby's life?" she asked.

All right, the wording was terrible. As a lawyer, she probably should have come up with something that wouldn't have lit a new fire in Aiden's eyes. And this time, the fire wasn't from the heat of that stupid morning kiss. She'd riled him again.

Aiden didn't exactly jump to answer. Perhaps because he was mulling over what to sling back at her. But he didn't get a chance to say or sling anything. The fluorescent lights flickered, snapping and crackling above them, before they clicked off.

Since there were no windows, the room instantly went pitch-black.

Kendall reached for Aiden's arm, but he was already reaching for her. "It'll be okay," he assured her. "The generator will kick right in."

There was no one else in the room with them, but Kendall heard one of the guards shout out some kind of code. Probably procedure for emergencies like this.

The seconds crawled by. There were more shouted orders from the guard. She recognized the voice as the same one who'd ushered them into the visiting area. She also heard footsteps scrambling around on the tile floors.

"Hell." Aiden got to his feet. "The power shouldn't be off this long."

Kendall agreed, but she didn't get a chance to voice it, because the alarms started clanging through the room. So loud. Much louder than a home security system, and the pulsing blare seemed to rattle the concrete block walls.

He pulled out his phone, cursed. It took her a moment to realize they had no cell service in this part of the building. The reinforced walls made it a dead zone for phone reception.

Aiden moved between her and the door, and even though she couldn't see him that well, she felt him automatically put his hand over his holster, but the gun wasn't there. He'd had to surrender it to the guard.

Her heart was already in her throat, and that didn't help. Was this some kind of prison break?

As far as she knew, Jewell was the only murder suspect on the women's side of the jail, but this wasn't Club Med, and there were other inmates who'd been charged and in some cases convicted of serious felonies.

They waited for what seemed an eternity and finally heard footsteps headed their way. Kendall pulled in her breath, held it, and the door creaked open. It was the bald guard, and he had a flashlight in his left hand, his gun in his right.

"Follow me," he barked.

But Aiden didn't jump to do that. "Why hasn't the generator kicked in?"

"A malfunction." He glanced back over his shoulder. "Now come on. I need to get you two out of here."

Still, Aiden didn't move. "What was your name again?"

Judging from the huff the guy made, he didn't like that question. Kendall wasn't sure she did, either. She wanted to get out of there, but she also wanted to make sure Jewell was okay. After all, this was the guard who was supposed to be bringing her to them. Did that mean Jewell was outside her cell in the dark where she could be hurt if this was indeed a prison break?

"Who are you?" Aiden repeated.

But he didn't answer.

The guard took aim and fired at them.

AIDEN BARELY HAD time to react.

Just as the shot cracked through the air, he pushed Kendall out of the way, praying that he hadn't hurt her in the process. He wasn't hit, and he launched himself at the guard. It was the best he could do, since he wasn't armed, and Aiden somehow had to stop him from firing again.

Aiden collided with the guy who was a heck of a lot bigger than he was, but it was thankfully enough to off-balance the gorilla, because they both crashed to the floor. The flashlight went flying, but the guard managed to hang on to his gun. It didn't help when the guard slugged him.

Damn, that hurt, and Aiden could have sworn he saw stars.

What the heck was going on here?

Clearly, this was a rogue guard, maybe involved in a prison outbreak. But why had he shot at them? Maybe because Aiden was the county sheriff?

He didn't have much time to dwell on that, because he got another punch to the face. Aiden landed a couple of punches as well, but what he couldn't seem to do was knock that gun out of the guard's hand.

The guard cursed him. Profanity that Aiden gave right

back to him, and the struggle landed outside the visiting room and into the small caged booth where the guards waited during visits. Normally, there were plenty of lights and security cameras, but it was now as dark as the rest of the facility.

Even over the sounds of the struggle and the blare of the alarm, Aiden could hear a voice coming from the communicator clipped to the guard's collar. He didn't hear every word, but Aiden caught enough to realize this guy had some help.

"The plug's been pulled. Get out of there now!" the voice said.

The guard cursed him again and kicked like a mule to get Aiden off him. He scrambled to his feet, turning to fire another shot. Aiden had no choice but to dart out of the way.

And it was just enough for the guard to sprint right out of the booth.

Aiden wanted to go after him, to pulverize the moron for the attack, but he wouldn't dare leave Kendall alone. Especially as she might have been hurt. That gave him another jolt of adrenaline. He scooped up the flashlight and hurried back to the visiting room.

He didn't have to look hard for Kendall. She was right there in the doorway. She'd picked up a chair and was holding it like some kind of weapon. Thank God she hadn't tried to use it on the guard, because he would likely have shot her.

"Let's go," Aiden said. Balancing the flashlight, he managed to get her death grip off the chair.

"Is it safe?" she asked, her voice trembling like the rest of her.

"I'll make it safe."

That was possibly a flat-out lie, but Kendall had already been through enough to hear the truth. A truth that didn't matter, since he didn't have a lot of options here. It definitely wasn't safe for them to stay in a room where they could be trapped—again. Their best shot was to get the heck out of Dodge.

"Stay low and behind me," Aiden ordered.

He turned the flashlight to the floor and got them moving. Slowly. And he tried to pick through all the shadows and sounds to figure out what was going on. He didn't dare call out for the guards because they might be on the bald guy's side. But in addition to looking out for rogue guards, he also needed to make sure Kendall and he weren't attacked by escaping prisoners.

Because the security booth was now empty, Aiden paused there and used the flashlight to locate his weapons and to check the hall to his left. It led to the cells, and if he remembered correctly, there were eight prisoners there in the women's wing. On the men's side, there was triple that number.

While he could hear hurried footsteps, there were no gunshots. That was something at least. Kendall had already dodged enough bullets to last a lifetime.

"This way," Aiden instructed.

He'd take Kendall up the main hall, to the next security checkpoint. After that, it wouldn't be much farther to get her out of the building. However, they'd made it only a few steps when he heard a voice.

"No!" someone shouted.

"Jewell," Kendall immediately said, and she would have bolted in that direction if Aiden hadn't held her back.

"It could be an ambush," he reminded her.

She frantically shook her head. "But she might need our help."

Or she could be the reason Kendall and he needed help in the first place.

Something about that didn't ring true for him, though. If Jewell had planned an escape from jail, she wouldn't have involved Kendall. Not like this. And that guard had fired a shot at them. The guy could have just run off, but he'd come after them. That likely meant this wasn't Jewell's plan.

But then, whose sick plan was it?

"We can't just leave my sister here," Kendall argued. "That guard could go after her."

True. At the moment, though, Aiden wasn't nearly as concerned about that as he was about Kendall's safety. Still, it was clear he wasn't going to get her out of there until he found Jewell.

Cursing the potential *damned if you do, damned if you don't* situation, Aiden reminded Kendall again to stay behind him, and he raced toward the hall where he'd heard Jewell's shouted no.

Thankfully, it didn't take Aiden long to spot her. With her blond hair and pale skin, she looked like a ghost in the shadows. She was cuffed, no guard in sight, and it appeared that she was trying to make her way toward them.

"Kendall!" she said, rushing toward her sister. Kendall did some rushing of her own, and she pulled Jewell into her arms. "The guard's going to try to kill you," Jewell warned them.

"Yeah, we know," Aiden confirmed.

What he wanted to find out, though, was how Jewell knew, but this wasn't exactly the time for questions. Especially since he was going to try to get out of this lethal tinderbox with a cuffed murder suspect and a woman who was already sporting one gunshot wound.

"Follow me," he said to them.

Huddled together, they did just that. Aiden tried to keep watch all around them. Hard to do with the darkness and the rooms that seemed to jut out from every direction.

Every step caused his heart to pound even harder, and that didn't improve when he got to the checkpoint and spotted the guard. Just in case this was the bald guy's partner, Aiden lifted his gun.

"I'm Sheriff Braddock," he announced.

The young guard whirled around and nearly lost his footing. If this was a partner in crime, then he sucked at it, because the kid was shaking more than Kendall was.

"What's going on?" Aiden asked him.

"Somebody tampered with the generator. That new fella, I think, because he just went tearing out of here."

Hell. The guy was getting away, no doubt, and Aiden really didn't want that to happen. Not that he had a lot of choices here.

"Where are the rest of the guards?" Aiden pressed.

"Some are trying to get that generator going and get everything locked down. The rest are in the cell blocks. We got some bad people down there."

Yes, and one of them was right behind him.

"The front door was open," the guard went on. "The new guy left it that way. I just locked it, but you got any idea how many regs it breaks to leave that door open?"

Plenty.

But an open door only meant the rogue and any of his helpers would have an easier time getting to Kendall for round two.

"I'm transporting this prisoner to the sheriff's office for questioning," Aiden let the man know. Not exactly standard procedure, but this was a protocol-bending situation if ever there was one. "Unlock the front door for me."

Aiden didn't wait to get his permission to leave. He

got Jewell and Kendall moving again up the hall and toward the front exit. However, he did spare Jewell a glance.

"If you try to escape, I'll make you pay," Aiden warned her.

Jewell blinked, as if that'd been the last thing on her mind. Maybe it was, but it was best to make that crystal clear.

"Just keep Kendall safe," Jewell said, her voice as thin and ghostly as the rest of her.

That was exactly what he planned to do.

The moment the guard unlocked the door, Aiden lifted his gun and with Jewell and Kendall in tow, he ran toward his truck.

Chapter Nine

The nightmare came again, and Kendall woke with a jolt. And she immediately groaned.

The sharp movement caused the stitches in her arm to pull, and she got an instant reminder of the pain. It wasn't as bad as it had been, but coupled with the images from the nightmare, it was more than she could take.

She looked down at the floor, expecting to see Aiden, knowing that just a glimpse of him would steady her nerves.

But he wasn't there.

Instead of steadied nerves, Kendall got another jolt of fear and adrenaline before she heard the water running in the adjoining bathroom. Aiden was apparently in the shower. Probably for the best. It would give her a moment to regain her composure and try to come to grips with the nightmare.

About her sister.

In the dream, Jewell hadn't made it out of that jail alive. The bald guard had succeeded in killing her. But it was just a nightmare. Jewell was very much alive and temporarily in the jail over in Silver Creek, a town not too far from Sweetwater Springs. Even though the warden had wanted Jewell returned within hours after regaining control of the county jail, Aiden had refused, citing his concern for her sister's safety.

Kendall was thankful beyond words for that.

Yes, Jewell was still in a cell, but Kendall figured she'd be a lot safer there than at the county jail. She knew the Ryland brothers, who were the lawmen in Silver Creek, and they'd protect her sister until other arrangements could be made. Of course, the Silver Creek Jail didn't have the right security level for the county to agree to keep Jewell there for long, but it was better than turning Jewell right back over to the warden before a thorough investigation of the security breach could be carried out.

She hadn't had a chance to talk to Jewell about the baby. Soon, though, Jewell would have to know exactly what had gone on between Aiden and her, and Kendall wanted to be the one to tell her.

When she heard Aiden turn off the shower, she got out of bed and put on her robe. She was wearing her pj's again, but with Aiden around, the more clothes, the better.

Aiden, however, didn't play by the rule of the wearing more clothes.

He came out of the bathroom, toweling his hair. No shirt. No boots. He had on his jeans, but they were only partially zipped. And goodness, he smelled like soap and sex. Her soap at that, but it smelled a heck of a lot better on him than her.

Since she was certain she was just standing there ogling him again, Kendall darted past him and went into the bathroom.

The room smelled like him, too.

She didn't shower. Didn't want to strip down and step into the shower where he'd just been. It might cause her to go running to him and beg him to join her. Instead Kendall washed up, brushed her teeth and forced herself not to put on makeup. Like her more-clothes rule, no makeup might make him take one look at her and decide their lustful past was over.

Or not.

That was certainly not a chaste look she got from him when she went back into the room. He was sitting on the foot of her bed again, still only partially dressed, and now he had his phone sandwiched against his shoulder and appeared to be talking to Leland. However, when he looked up, their gazes met.

And just like that, she was lost.

Good grief.

Since it wasn't a smart idea for her to stay there and risk another kiss, Kendall headed downstairs to the kitchen to take her prenatal vitamin and have a glass of milk. Since she'd gotten pregnant, the taste of coffee made her queasy, but she started a pot for Aiden.

She heard him coming down the stairs, his footsteps echoing in the empty house, and Kendall tried to prepare herself for the sight of him. She would have had an easier time stopping a tornado with a paper fan.

He was now wearing a shirt, thank goodness, one from the clothes he'd had a deputy pick up from his house and bring to him. There was nothing special about the dark gray shirt or his jeans, other than the fact that Aiden was the one wearing them.

"There should be some kind of cure for you," she mumbled.

Obviously, she didn't mumble it softly enough, because he heard, and the corner of his mouth lifted. For a split second anyway. Then he followed the smile with a scowl, no doubt reminding himself that this attraction was only going to get them in more trouble.

And trouble came her way.

Aiden slipped his phone into his pocket and studied her as if trying to figure out what he should do or say about her mumblings.

"Anything wrong at the Silver Creek Jail?" she asked.

He shook his head. "Your sister's fine."

That was it. All the conversation he apparently intended, because Aiden cursed, slipped his hand around the back of her neck and pulled her to him. Before her breasts even landed against his chest, his mouth was on her.

And he tasted so good.

It wasn't fair that with just one little kiss, he could send her body into such a tailspin.

He was fighting it, she could tell. The muscles in his arms were stiff. His hands, too, but he didn't back away. Instead, with his mouth still on hers, he groaned and deepened the kiss.

So not good.

Well, not good for their situation, but Kendall soon forgot all about that. There was no booze involved in this kiss. No quick peck like yesterday to get back at him for his snark. This was all heat.

Kendall hadn't intended to move, but she soon found her lower back pressed against the counter. With Aiden pressed against her. Everything fit, of course. His strong arms around her. Body to body. With his right leg wedged between hers.

His scent coiled around her. Mingling with the heat and the pressure that his leg was creating. The right pressure in the right place.

Which made it incredibly wrong.

The pregnancy was going to be plenty hard enough for their families to handle. They didn't need to add an affair to it.

Thankfully, that was enough to get her to unravel herself from his arms. Her body didn't thank her for it, but it was the right thing to do.

Kendall repeated that to herself.

Her body wasn't quite buying it, though, and with Aiden standing in front of her looking like the hottest of her hot fantasies, it took everything inside her to step away from him.

"My hormones are all out of whack," she said. Of course, they usually were when she was within ten feet of Aiden.

"Hormones," he repeated, sounding skeptical.

With good reason. Pregnancy hormones didn't have anything to do with this, and for a moment Aiden looked as if he might prove that to her with yet another kiss. But hopefully he wouldn't. Because Kendall didn't think she had enough willpower to resist another onslaught from that sizzling mouth of his.

Since the coffee was ready, it seemed like a good time to pour him a cup. "What did Leland have to say? Are there any updates?" Something she should already have asked him along with any other question she could come up with fast.

"I need to apologize for that kiss first," he grumbled.

But Kendall waved him off. "We've been apologizing for kisses for over twenty years now."

And it was the truth.

Twenty-three years. A lifetime to be lusting after Aiden, and the memory of that first kiss came flooding back. The news of his father's disappearance had just hit. No details yet of the blood in the cabin. Only the speculations, gossip and questions as to why Whitt was gone.

In those days the Braddocks had lived close enough to the McKinnons, and Kendall had ridden her horse over there to check on Aiden. He'd said he was fine. But he hadn't been. Even as a young girl, she'd been able to see that, and she had put her arms around him to try to comfort him.

The kiss had happened there in the barn with the smell of the hay and horses. If she'd known that just a couple of days later her sister would be whisking her away, Kendall would have made that kiss last a lot longer.

He stayed quiet a moment. "Yeah." And he gulped down some coffee as if it were the cure for what ailed him. "But we were young and stupid back then. Now we're just stupid."

Kendall couldn't help it, she laughed. Aiden stared at her as if she'd lost it, but then the corner of his mouth lifted. "It was clumsy but effective," he said.

It took her a moment to realize he was talking about that kiss. An apt description for it. Her braces hadn't helped, that was for sure, but that twenty-three-year-old kiss had stayed with her all this time.

A benchmark of sorts.

Too bad no other man had quite lived up to it.

A truly sad thought.

"Palmer's already out of jail on bond," Aiden tossed out there.

Since her mind was still on the kiss, it took her a moment to switch gears. "You knew his lawyers wouldn't let him stay there long." She paused. "But there's something else, isn't there?"

He had another sip of coffee first. "Leland said Palmer went off on him. Yelling and cursing. Leland seems to think if Palmer hasn't already done something crazy, he will."

Yes, that definitely qualified as *something else*. "He could have been the one to orchestrate that attack at the jail."

But why? The attack definitely seemed to have been aimed at Aiden and her, and while Palmer didn't care much for Aiden, he'd never had anything against her.

Unless…

"What if Palmer thinks I can connect the missing kidnapper back to him?" she asked.

Aiden shook his head. "How could you do that?"

"Well, I admitted to Joplin that there was something familiar about the guy. Something I couldn't quite put my finger on. Maybe Palmer doesn't want me to remember the man because it'll connect to him."

"The same can be said for Joplin," Aiden reminded her.

She couldn't argue with that. "When I talk to Jewell about the baby, I also want to tell her our suspicions about Joplin. She might fire him and hire someone else. Of course, that wouldn't be smart with Jewell's trial so close, but if Joplin had anything to do with these attacks, then I don't want him anywhere near my sister. Jewell would feel the same way about me."

Well, maybe.

"Bingo," Aiden said as if reading her mind. "Jewell won't like that I've gotten you pregnant."

Take a number. Plenty of people weren't going to like it.

Aiden stared at her from over the rim of his cup. "I'm not going to walk away from this baby."

"Even if it causes a rift in your family?" she asked.

"Even then," he answered just as quickly.

He sounded so confident, and Kendall immediately got a dose of another fantasy. Aiden and her raising their son together. A little boy who'd look just like his daddy with that sandy-blond hair and those mood-changing gray eyes. Since it was a fantasy she'd had most of her life, it wasn't hard to consider it now.

And dismiss it.

"You're talking about shared custody?" she asked.

Aiden stared at her again. Then nodded.

Okay. Not ideal in the fantasy department. Heck, not even ideal in the real world, because she'd wanted to raise her child herself. She definitely didn't want him to be shuffled from one house to another the way she had been as a child. Her parents had divorced shortly after she was born, and Kendall had often felt pulled between her mom and her dad.

She hadn't wanted that for her baby.

Before Kendall could ask Aiden how he thought such an arrangement would play out, his phone rang, and she saw Leland's name on the screen. She hoped the deputy wasn't calling with bad news about Jewell or some plan that Palmer had to get back at them.

Aiden didn't put the call on speaker, and he actually stepped away from her only seconds after his conversation started with the deputy. Not a good sign. Neither was Aiden's forehead, which bunched up.

"When and where?" Aiden asked.

Kendall moved closer to see if she could hear anything Leland was saying. She couldn't. So she could only stand there and wait.

"What's the COD?" Aiden continued a moment later.

That caused her breath to go thin. COD was cause of death. Oh, God. What had happened now?

By the time Aiden finished the call, Kendall's heart was in her throat. "It's not Jewell," she managed to say.

"No." He put away his phone, reached out and touched her arm. "It's the bald guard. His name is Deacon Lynch, and his body was found in a wooded area just off the interstate. He died from gunshot wounds to the head."

Her breath rushed out. Pure relief. Jewell was okay.

But it didn't take long for the obvious question to come to her. "Who killed him?"

Aiden shook his head. "No sign of anyone but the dead body. He was shot at point-blank range."

Even though she wasn't a criminal trial attorney, Kendall was familiar enough with police investigations to know what that meant. "Lynch probably knew his killer."

"Yeah, and his killer is likely the person who hired him. Maybe to silence him so he wouldn't talk."

Of course. The guard had botched the attack and was on the run. His boss wouldn't have wanted him trying to work out a plea deal with the cops. Too bad. Because a plea deal could have given them information so they could put an end to the danger and lock up the monster behind these attacks.

"It's not over," Kendall heard herself mumble, heading out of the kitchen. "I should get dressed so I can visit Jewell."

And then the blasted tears threatened.

She'd already cried way too much, and it only made things worse because it put an even more troubled look in Aiden's eyes. He was worried enough about the safety of the baby and their situation, and now he had to be concerned about how this stress was affecting the pregnancy.

Aiden caught up with her in the foyer. As he'd done earlier, he cursed. Then reached out for her. No kiss this time, but he tugged her away from the door and the two sidelight windows. He didn't stop there. Aiden pulled her into his arms and tucked her head beneath his chin.

"You don't seem to have a lot of faith in my abilities as a sheriff," he said.

Maybe that was meant to lighten the mood. She did have faith in him, because Aiden was a good cop, but someone wanted them dead. And the worst part? Kendall wasn't even sure why.

He brushed a kiss on the top of her head. And the heat came again. Not that it'd ever completely gone away, but it gave her another slam of a reminder she didn't need.

"I should change," she said, but she didn't move. Her feet were anchored to the floor.

Aiden made a sound of agreement, but he didn't move, either.

Heck, she had to do something. "If you kiss me again, you know where it will lead."

Straight to the bedroom.

Another sound of agreement from him, and he leaned his head back. Enough to make eye contact with her. Brief eye contact. Then wham.

Another kiss.

Oh, mercy. This wasn't going to stop.

Well, not stop with just a kiss anyway. Kendall definitely felt the difference between this one and the other. Both were scalding hot, but this one had some urgency to it, and even though Aiden was trying to be gentle, he seemed to be losing that battle, too.

It was a battle she just might have let him win.

If she hadn't heard the sound.

Aiden heard it as well, and he whipped toward the door, shoving her behind him in the same motion.

It didn't take long for Kendall to see the source of the sound. There, on the front porch peering through the side-light window, she spotted their visitor.

Aiden's mother.

And it was clear from Carla's glare that she'd seen exactly what Kendall and Aiden had been doing.

"Open up," Carla shouted. "We need to talk *now*."

Chapter Ten

Aiden groaned. He definitely didn't need his mother's visit this morning. Neither did Kendall, but she stepped away from him, disengaged the security system and opened the door so his mother could come in.

From just the sound of her voice, Aiden had already known that Carla was in a snit, but without the glass between them, he could see every bit of that fury in her eyes.

"You were kissing her," Carla snapped.

"Yes," Aiden admitted. "Last I heard, that wasn't a crime."

Though he knew Carla would put it on the same level as a felony. Ditto for some members of Kendall's family, too.

"We just got upsetting news," Kendall explained, obviously trying to make this better.

But there was nothing she could say to do that, and that was why Aiden stepped between them. He closed the door, too, just in case whoever had killed the prison guard was waiting out there with a high-powered rifle.

"And kissing my son makes bad news better?" Carla fired back.

"Yes," Kendall said after a long pause. "As a matter of fact, it did help."

Aiden nearly laughed. Kendall had some backbone

all right, but it wasn't a trait that Carla was going to appreciate right now.

Every muscle in Carla's jaw turned to iron, and she aimed the next glare at him. "So, now you're staying here with her?"

He nodded. "Someone's tried to kill Kendall twice. She's pregnant with my baby, and I want to be able to make sure she's safe."

Of course, so far he was doing a lousy job of that, but Aiden swore to himself that he'd do better.

"One of your deputies could have stayed with her," Carla argued. "Or one of Jewell's sons."

Aiden put his hand on Kendall's stomach. "This is my baby," he clarified, knowing he sounded smart-mouthed in the process. "I've got more at stake here than my deputies or the McKinnons."

"Well, I don't like it." Carla's glare got worse.

No surprise there. Aiden didn't like a lot of things about this—her visit included.

"Why are you here, Mother?" he asked.

Even with the direct question, she still didn't take those glaring eyes off Kendall and him. She finally reached into her enormous purse, pulled out a padded envelope and handed it to him.

"I have some evidence against Robert Joplin," Carla said. "It should be enough for you to arrest him for these attacks."

You could have knocked Aiden over with a feather, and judging from the slight gasp Kendall made, she was equally shocked.

"What kind of evidence?" Aiden wanted to know. As the envelope wasn't sealed, he looked inside and saw a cell phone.

"There's a recording of Joplin meeting with a hired

gun." For having just delivered a bombshell, Carla stayed pretty calm. "If you dig around, I think you can link it to the man who kidnapped Kendall."

Okay. That would be nice if that truly happened, but Aiden had his doubts. "How'd you get this?"

Now she dodged his gaze. "I hired a PI to follow Joplin, and he managed to record it."

Aiden gave her a flat look. "Did this PI you hired break any laws to get it?"

Carla lifted her shoulder, managed to look a little indignant. "What does it matter? It's practically a confession."

"It matters. If the PI obtained it illegally like with a wiretap, then I can't use it to arrest Joplin." However, it would be proof of the lawyer's guilt, so maybe it would give Aiden a jumping-off point to launch an investigation.

He looked at Kendall to see how she was handling this, but she shook her head. "If Joplin's guilty, I want him to fry."

So did Aiden.

Since the phone had already been compromised for prints while in his mother's purse and heaven knew where else, Aiden took it out and clicked the button to hear the recording. The quality was far from ideal, but he had no trouble hearing the voices of two men.

"You'll get half the money now and half when the job's done," Joplin said.

"You want it done at her place?" the second man asked.

"It doesn't matter," Joplin answered. "Just get it done."

And that was it.

While it wasn't exactly a confession of guilt, it certainly sounded suspicious. Still, there was a big problem. "Joplin could say he was talking to his gardener or any other employee that he was sending to somebody's house to do work."

His mother handed him a piece of paper she took from her purse. "That's the name of the man on the recording. Barry McNease. If you check, you'll find he has a long criminal record."

Aiden would check all right, but he had some other things to settle first. "I'll need the name of the PI who did the recording," he said to Carla.

She hesitated and finally extracted a business card from her purse. "I don't know why you just can't see this recording as a gift to get a guilty man off the streets."

"I'd rather be sure that this *gift* isn't just some trumped-up nonsense designed to send the wrong man to jail. Arresting the wrong person won't keep Kendall safe."

Aiden paused and went on to the next matter he needed clarified. "I had a chat with Joplin yesterday, and he said you're the one who told him Kendall was pregnant."

Carla pulled back her shoulders as if she might launch into a denial. Then she shrugged. "I told him because I thought maybe Jewell and he could talk some sense into Kendall."

"Excuse me?" Kendall didn't stay behind him. She came out to face his mother head-on. "What's your definition of talking some sense into me?"

Carla's gaze darted around for a few uncomfortable seconds. "You shouldn't be raising a child. Your sister's a killer, and your blood is the same as hers."

"Alleged killer," Aiden corrected. He was glad Kendall wasn't the hitting, hair-pulling type, because his mother had just crossed a very big line. "That's why we have courts of law and such."

"And you think you'd be a better person to raise my baby?" Kendall asked Carla, but she didn't wait for an answer. "Because you're not. You're a bitter woman, and you have no say whatsoever in my life or this child's."

Aiden hoped like the devil that the *no say* didn't apply to him, too. But it was clear this visit was not making things better. Well, maybe with the exception of the recording, but there were so many possible snags that went along with it that it would likely turn out to be nothing. Still, before he ushered his mother out, he had one more question for her.

"How did you even know Kendall was pregnant?" Aiden demanded. "And this time I want the truth."

Carla looked him straight in the eye. "Your sister told me."

"Laine," Kendall said on a huff.

"No. Shelby," Carla corrected. Her chin came up. "That horrible Lee Palmer hired PIs to follow all of us around so he could get some dirt to help out Jewell. Shelby found out about it and started following one of the PIs. She saw you two leave the Bluebonnet together three months ago."

"Wait a minute. The PI that Palmer hired was following me?" Kendall asked.

"Or maybe Aiden. Shelby wasn't sure, so she stuck close to him and then followed you to the hotel. We'd both hoped the one-night stand would be the end of it between you two. We were obviously wrong."

Yep. They'd been wrong. But now Aiden knew how the word had gotten around about Kendall and him at the bar. Either his sister had blabbed it. Or maybe the PI. Maybe even Carla once she got the info from Shelby.

"That doesn't explain how you knew I was pregnant," Kendall said to his mother.

"I'm not sure how Shelby found out, but she's the one who told me." With that, Carla turned to leave, and like a child who'd just gotten scolded, she slammed the door behind her.

"I think it's time I had a little chat with Shelby," Aiden said.

He put the phone with the recording on the stairs and took out his own cell. He also motioned for Kendall to lock the door and reset the alarm.

"I can put the call on speaker," he said to Kendall. "But it's highly probable that my sister will say some things you won't like."

"I already know what people are saying. Please put the call on speaker."

Aiden did, but he hoped he didn't regret it. Especially as Kendall had already had enough ill will thrown at her this morning.

"What?" Shelby snapped when she answered the call. Obviously, he'd woken her, but Aiden didn't care. His sister had some serious explaining to do.

"So you followed Kendall and me?" Aiden demanded.

Shelby made a sleepy, irritated sound. "Just Kendall. Well, actually I followed a PI who was following Kendall, but since you were with her, let's just say you got caught up in the net."

Thankfully, Kendall didn't snap about that being a violation of her privacy, because if Shelby knew she was listening, she might not be so willing to answer his questions. But if she didn't supply those answers now, she *would* give them to him. One way or another.

"So you followed Kendall, you found out that we'd spent the night together in the hotel and you spilled it to Laine and then Mom," Aiden recapped.

"They told you that?"

"Mom did. I just had a *friendly* chat with her about it. You might have given me a heads-up, Shelby."

"I hadn't meant to tell her. It just sort of slipped out. But while we're doing the finger-pointing, you should have told me that you were messing around with the likes of Kendall O'Neal."

Kendall gave a heavy sigh, stepped away and would have headed to the sidelight window, no doubt to look out to make sure his mother was gone. But Aiden didn't want her in any potential gunman's line of sight, so he held her back.

"Aiden, I can't believe you slept with her," Shelby added.

He reminded himself that he loved his sister. Not right at the moment. But in a big picture kind of way, he loved her. "It happened. Now Kendall's pregnant and in danger. What do you know about that?"

Silence. For a very long time. "When you talked to Mom, did she seem, well, okay?"

That definitely wasn't a question that Aiden had expected. "No. But then she never seems okay. She's been in a bad mood for twenty-three years." And seeing a shrink. "Why? Does she seem okay to you?"

More silence. "I'm not sure. Something was off."

"I can say the same thing about you," Aiden countered. "Why exactly did you follow the PI?"

"Because I want to make sure Jewell's convicted, that's why," Shelby answered.

Aiden's huff matched Kendall's. "There's a boatload of evidence against Jewell," he reminded his sister. "Lots of Dad's blood in the cabin. Jewell's DNA on the sheets. Those bone fragments found just a stone's throw away from the cabin. Sounds like a slam dunk to me."

Well, with the exception of a confession.

And the niggling feeling Aiden was getting that this

particular slam dunk seemed to be tied up into a too-neat package.

But maybe that was the fault of the pregnancy. And the kissing session. Or just being around Kendall.

"I don't want any questions in the jury's mind of Jewell's guilt," Shelby continued. "Jewell weighs a hundred and ten pounds soaking wet, and Daddy was a big man. I figure she must have had help moving the body from the cabin to the creek."

That had come up plenty of times, and most folks thought Jewell's husband, Roy, had helped. But an eyewitness had recently cleared Roy.

"So you're looking at possible accessories to a murder?" Aiden concluded.

"Yes. Joplin and Palmer are tops on my list. From everything I've learned, Joplin was in love with Jewell even back then. And we both know how much Palmer hated Daddy."

Aiden made a sound of agreement. "Am I on your list? I was big enough to have helped move a body, and Dad and I weren't exactly on friendly terms, either."

Shelby made a garbled sound of outrage and shock. "What the heck does that mean?"

"It means that not everything about this case is black-and-white." And he waited, figuring that would prompt an argument or maybe Shelby would bring up that he was going soft because of the baby.

But his sister stayed quiet. Quiet enough for Aiden so that the niggling feeling became even worse.

"Mom gave me the recording with Joplin and an alleged scumbag who might have been hired to kidnap Kendall," Aiden explained, hoping to squish that feeling. "She said she got it from a PI she hired, but I'm assuming you gave it to her."

"Well, you're assuming wrong." Shelby paused again. "What's on this recording?"

"Maybe nothing. I need to talk to Joplin about it." And Aiden figured the lawyer would try to explain it away just as Palmer had tried to do with the traffic camera footage.

"Joplin has plenty of motive to want those bone fragments destroyed," Shelby insisted.

So did others. But that brought Aiden to something he wanted to make crystal clear. "Shelby, you need to back off from this investigation."

"What—"

Aiden talked right over her howling protest. "Here's the deal. What you're doing could be construed as interfering with a murder investigation and possibly even the judicial process. Do you really want to give Joplin a reason to file a motion to have the case against Jewell thrown out?"

"He'd have no grounds for that," she fired back.

"And don't give him any. Back off, Shelby, and that's not brotherly advice, that's a warning from the county sheriff."

Aiden braced himself for an argument, something that Shelby was darn good at, but more of that unsettling silence followed.

"Are you and Kendall okay?" Shelby finally asked. "I heard about the attack at the jail. It sounds as if you two could have been hurt."

Her concern for Kendall was a little surprising. And welcome. "We could have been killed. I don't guess in all your digging around that anything came up about a scumbag prison guard on the take?"

Oh, man.

It was suddenly quiet enough to hear a pin drop.

"All right, what the heck is wrong?" Aiden demanded.

"Maybe nothing," Shelby said almost in a whisper.

That got Aiden groaning because it not only confirmed that something was indeed wrong but that it was something Shelby didn't like.

"It's about Mom," Shelby finally said.

Kendall pulled in her breath, moved closer to the phone. Aiden held his breath, too, because he was a hundred percent certain this was something he wasn't going to like.

"I think we can agree that Mom's been acting a little erratic lately," Shelby continued. "She's upset about the baby."

Heck, no. He did *not* like the direction this was going.

"What the hell did she do?" Aiden growled.

Shelby cleared her throat. "When I was at the house last night, I saw a bank statement on her personal computer. Not for her regular bank. This was one I didn't know about."

Strange, since Shelby managed the family's finances and Carla's trust fund.

"I told Mom about the baby four days ago," Shelby went on, "and twenty-four hours later, she withdrew a large sum of money from this account that I didn't even know she had."

That put a tight knot in his stomach. "How much?"

"Fifty thousand," Shelby admitted after yet another pause. "I hoped maybe she was planning a big trip or something, so after dinner I asked her about it. She claimed she didn't know what I was talking about. When I went back to her office to show her, the account had been deleted, and there was no trace of it. I can't think of a good reason why Mom would do something like that, can you?"

No, but he could think of a bad one.

Apparently, Kendall could, too.

"Oh, God," Kendall whispered, and she pressed her fingers to her mouth.

And Aiden knew why. Fifty thousand dollars was plenty enough to pay for the attacks on Kendall.

"I have to go," Aiden said to Shelby. "I need to talk to our mother now."

He pushed the end call button, but before Aiden could scroll through for Carla's number, his phone rang. At first he thought it was Shelby calling back to tell him to go easy on their mom.

But unknown caller was on the screen.

That knot in his gut tightened.

"Sheriff Braddock," Aiden answered. He didn't put the call on speaker, but Kendall moved so close that she'd likely hear anyway.

There was a lot of static on the line, and it took several seconds before the caller said anything. "This is Harry Yost."

Aiden looked at Kendall to see if she knew who that was, but she only shook her head.

"Who are you and what do you want?" Aiden asked the man. He didn't bother to sound friendly, either, because there were rarely good reasons why someone didn't want their number viewed.

"I'm the person who kidnapped Kendall O'Neal and took her to your place," the man volunteered. "If you want to find out why I did that, then come and see me so we can talk."

Chapter Eleven

Kendall didn't have to ask the caller if he was lying about who he was. He wasn't. She recognized his voice. It was indeed one of the men who'd kidnapped her.

And the very one who'd shot her.

He had also tried to kill Aiden and her before getting away in the SUV. Because he'd been missing for two days, she'd thought that maybe they'd seen the last of him. Apparently not.

"I'm listening," Aiden said, pressing the speaker button so she could hear better. Probably because she was right against him, and he needed to take out a small notepad and pen from his pocket.

"Don't bother trying to trace the call," Yost said. "I'm using a burner, and I'll toss it as soon as we're done talking."

Maybe they'd get some answers before that happened. "Why me?" Kendall asked.

"Can't answer that. I got orders to take you and use you to get the sheriff to destroy that evidence."

"Who gave you those orders?" Aiden demanded.

It sounded as if the guy chuckled. "Not gonna get into that over the phone. I'm looking for some help here, and I figure the only way I'll get that help is to have something I can use to barter."

Kendall hung on every word. Processing it and mentally repeating it. "I know you," she said.

Yost, if that was truly his name, didn't jump to verify that. "Our paths have crossed. When you were at the pharmacy waiting for your prescription to be filled, I started chatting to you about headache meds."

It took her a moment, but it all came back. A big guy, dark hair with a military cut. "You followed me there."

"I did." No trouble admitting it, and that fact caused Aiden to mumble some profanity. "My partner and I were supposed to take you from the parking lot, but somebody was following you. Thought it was wise for us to back off and take you from your office instead."

The someone following her had probably been the PI Palmer had hired. Or maybe it was the one working for Aiden's mother. There were an awful lot of PIs lurking around, and it turned her stomach to think that she hadn't noticed them. Of course, with the pregnancy and Jewell's trial, she'd had a lot on her mind.

That misstep had turned out to be dangerous.

"I thought you might have remembered my voice," Yost confirmed a moment later. "And that you maybe could have picked me out of a photo lineup."

"I could have. Is that why you tried to have me killed at the jail?" she asked.

"I had no part in that one, but I got caught up in the flak."

"How?" Aiden snapped. "And did you have something to do with the dead guard from the county jail?"

Silence. For a long time. "That's something for a face-to-face conversation, something I want to have with Miss O'Neal and you."

Aiden was shaking his head before Yost even finished. "I'm not letting Kendall get anywhere near you."

"You will if she wants to know who's trying to kill her. I'm at the football field at the high school in Clay Ridge. It's early, but there are plenty of kids already here for track practice. Some cheerleaders, too."

"Don't you hurt those kids," Aiden growled.

"Wouldn't dream of it. I just figured you'd be more inclined to visit with me if I made it in an *interesting* location."

His smugness made her want to reach through the phone and slap him. How dare he play with people's lives like this? And apparently he'd done it all for money, as Yost said someone had hired him.

"How do you think a meeting between us would play out?" she asked.

Aiden glared at her, letting her know with those narrowed eyes that such a meeting wasn't going to happen. Still, she wanted to know what this dirtbag expected of her.

"I'm thinking you'll show up here in a half hour," Yost went on. "Since you're probably still at your house over in Sweetwater Springs, that should give you enough time if you don't dawdle. Or if the sheriff doesn't take the time to drop you off somewhere."

Which was exactly what Aiden would do. No way would he let her go near this guy again after what he'd done to her the last time. Kendall could still hear the gunshot. Still feel the pain in her arm. And while she wanted to know the truth, she couldn't put her baby at risk.

Couldn't put Aiden at risk, either.

However, Kendall seriously doubted she'd be able to stop him from going to this meeting.

"Then what?" Aiden pressed. "You expect to tell me whatever it is you think I want to know and then just walk away?"

"No. I expect protective custody. The real kind where I'm, you know, actually protected and not shot or beat to death while I'm in a holding cell."

"You need protecting?" Aiden didn't sound any more convinced of that than she was. This guy was a killer. That said, the jail guard was dead, and it was likely that his killer wanted to do the same to Yost.

But why?

Why set this monster into motion and then kill him?

Maybe because she could identify him and somehow link him back to the person who hired him.

She glanced up at Aiden, their gazes meeting, and even though he didn't say anything to her, she figured he was on the same wavelength. Now Kendall needed to make the connection. And fast.

"Of course I need protecting," Yost finally said. "My partner, Montel Higgins, is dead. Don't want to end up like him… I gotta go," he quickly added. "I see somebody." No more smugness. Judging from his tone, he was scared. Or else he was pretending to be.

"Who do you see?" Aiden asked.

"Gotta go," Yost repeated. "Just get here fast, because in thirty minutes, I'm outta here." And with that, he hung up.

Kendall didn't waste a second. She headed straight for the stairs. "I'll get dressed."

"This doesn't mean you're coming with me," he called up to her, and she heard him start on some phone calls. Hopefully, arranging backup for himself so he wouldn't have to face Yost alone.

Kendall dressed as fast as she could, throwing on a pair of jeans and a top. When she made it back downstairs, Aiden was still on the phone, so she disengaged the security system. As he'd done other times, he looked around outside, finished his call and got her moving to his truck.

"I'll drop you off with Leland and Sarah at the sheriff's office," Aiden explained. "Jeb will go with me."

Jeb, the most inexperienced deputy in the department. That didn't help steady her nerves.

"Yost said you wouldn't have time to do that," she reminded him.

He gave her a determined glance. "You're staying with the deputies."

She wished that Aiden could do the same, stay tucked away safely with her, but Kendall knew she had zero chance of talking him out of this. After all, he was the sheriff, and he'd want to talk to Yost to see what he could learn.

And they had plenty to learn.

"What are you going to do about your mother?" she risked asking.

No look this time. Not at her anyway. Aiden kept watch around them. Still, she had no trouble seeing the muscles at war in his jaw. "I'll treat her like any other suspect."

From some people, that might have been lip service. It wasn't from Aiden. "Can you think of a reason why your mother would withdraw that money?"

A reason that didn't involve kidnapping her to force Aiden to destroy evidence.

A reason that didn't involve the baby, either.

"You know that my mother is seeing a shrink," he finally said. "Well, she needs it. I told you about her depression, but she's also been battling extreme mood swings since Dad was killed."

Another reminder of how many lives had been affected from that one tragic day.

"Did she have mental problems before?" Kendall asked, causing Aiden to give her a questioning glance.

Even though it'd been a simple question, apparently he knew that it hadn't come out of the blue.

"Before what? Did you find out something about my mother?" he asked.

That required a deep breath. "Maybe." And another deep breath. "Like Shelby, I've been doing plenty of research, and I came across an elderly woman who used to work for a psychiatrist. She said she thought your mother had been his patient a long time ago."

The surprise went through his eyes. "How long ago?"

"Before she married your father. But I don't have any other details," she added. "In fact, I'm not even sure it's true. The woman's almost eighty years old, and her memory might not be that good."

Kendall was clinging to that. Even if Carla had spent time there, she could see why the woman wouldn't want to share something like that with her kids. Still, if Carla had had issues for that long, then maybe those *issues* had resurfaced with news of the baby.

"Carla never mentioned it?" Kendall asked.

Aiden shook his head, and he sat there, stiff and silent as stone.

Kendall waited a few moments. Not nearly enough time for him to process all this, but they were just scratching at the surface and didn't have a lot of time to work this out.

"Of course, I now have to wonder about the money that Shelby saw in the account," Kendall added.

More silence, and he seemed to be trying to tamp down his nerves. "Carla might be hoping to use it as some kind of payoff to you. Maybe to get you to give up the baby."

Kendall's mouth fell open. "I'd never give up this baby. *Never.* Not for any amount of money—"

"I know that, but my mother's desperate, so she might be willing to do desperate things."

"How desperate?" she pressed when Aiden didn't continue.

He swallowed hard. "Desperate enough to try to get you out of the picture."

That caused her heart to slam against her chest. Of course, Kendall had already considered it after everything she'd learned, but it was another thing to hear it said aloud. From the woman's own son, no less.

"I'll handle it," Aiden went on. "I'll bring her in, question her. If she's behind this, I'll get the truth."

A truth that could shake him to the core. Yes, Aiden's relationship with his mother was rocky, but she was still his mother. And if she'd truly been behind the kidnapping, then that also meant she was responsible for the attempts to kill them.

Good God, had Carla tried to have her own son killed? Or was he just possible collateral damage, because Kendall would have been Carla's real target?

"I'm sorry." Kendall slipped her hand over his. More tight muscles. But he didn't pull away. "And it might not even be her. After all, we have two other suspects. Palmer and Joplin."

Aiden didn't answer, but she figured he was hoping that it was anybody but Carla.

His phone rang, and when he fished it from his pocket, she saw Leland's name on the screen again.

"We got a problem," Leland said the moment that Aiden answered. "There's been a report of gunshots near the high school."

Aiden cursed. "I'm still five minutes out."

"Sarah and I are on the way there now. I know that only leaves Jeb in the office to watch Kendall, so I called Seth Calder. He was at the jail going over what happened, and he'll be at the office by the time you get there."

Aiden groaned slightly but thanked Leland. His phone also beeped, indicating that he had another call coming in. One look at the screen, and Aiden cursed again when he saw it was from an unknown caller.

Yost, no doubt.

"I'll call you back," Aiden said to his deputy and then switched over to Yost. "What the hell's going on?"

"Well, it's not going as planned, that's for sure. Some-body's shooting at me, and I had to return fire." Yost sounded out of breath, as if he was running. And there was a loud bang. Probably the sound of another shot.

Oh, God. The students could be hurt.

"Who's shooting at you?" Aiden demanded.

"Don't know. Yet. But obviously there's been a change of plans. Don't come here. I'll call you when I'm out of this mess."

"My deputies are on the way to you now," Aiden told the man, but he was talking to the air, since Yost had al-ready hung up.

Aiden sped up even more, but he continued to keep watch around them, and when he reached the sheriff's of-fice, he didn't go into the parking lot. He literally drove onto the sidewalk so he could stop his truck directly in front of the entrance. Seth was already there, stepping out of his vehicle, and he hurried toward her.

"Tell Jeb to lock down the place," Aiden told Seth. "And thanks."

Seth grumbled a terse "you're welcome" and he got her inside. He didn't have to tell Jeb to do a lockdown, because the deputy started it right away.

Kendall looked out the reinforced window, praying that Aiden would be all right, but as soon as he put his truck in gear to drive away, she heard a sound that she didn't want to hear.

A gunshot.

And this wasn't coming from the school a mile away. It was close. So close that Seth pushed her behind him, drew his gun and looked out the window, as well. Kendall came up on her toes so she could look over his shoulder, but there was nothing to see. Not at first anyway.

There was another thick blast.

Followed by the sound of Aiden's truck door.

And a moment later, she saw Aiden peering around the edge of the building, his attention on the park behind the sheriff's office.

"The shooter's out there," she whispered, her voice already shaking. She wasn't worried for herself but for Aiden.

"Aiden's deputies are coming," Seth reminded her, no doubt sensing the bad scenarios going through her head. "He'll have backup soon."

But maybe soon wouldn't be soon enough.

There was another shot.

Mercy, who was doing this? Yost? Or was this the person he'd mentioned seeing at the school? She figured whoever that person was, he didn't have friendly intentions, because Yost had ended the call darn fast.

"Stay down." Seth looked back at her with a warning glance. "The glass is bullet-resistant, but a cop-killer bullet can get through. Sorry," he added in a mumble when she gasped.

Cop-killer. A coated bullet that could penetrate walls. And kill cops like Aiden.

"I just don't want you hurt," Seth said to her. "And neither does Aiden."

That was true, but that still didn't level her breathing. Why was this happening again?

"I'm Sheriff Braddock," Aiden called out to the shooter. "Drop your weapon."

That didn't happen. There was a fourth shot. Thankfully, it didn't seem to come Aiden's way, but he was out there and could be gunned down.

"There," Seth said. He used his gun to motion toward a cluster of trees that were about thirty yards from the building.

At first Kendall didn't see anything, but then there was a blur of motion. Someone running from one tree to the other. However, she couldn't tell if it was Yost. Maybe it was an innocent bystander just trying to get out of the way of those bullets.

Kendall pulled in her breath. Waiting and praying. The seconds crawled by, turning into one very long minute. No more shots. No more blurs of motion.

"The deputies are here," Seth told her.

But when Kendall tried to see, he blocked her way again.

"They're just up the street," he added.

Good. Hopefully, just their arrival would cause the shooter or Yost to back off. If Yost was indeed the one doing the shooting, that is.

Just as that thought crossed her mind, someone fired. The shot seemed even louder than the others. Judging from the way Seth's shoulders tensed, the bullet had come closer to the building.

It was the same for the next shot.

But that bullet sounded different. It took Kendall a

moment to realize why. It was the sound of a shot hitting someone.

"Aiden?" she called out and would have bolted to the door if Seth hadn't caught on to her.

"You can't go out there," he insisted.

Yes, she knew that. She couldn't put the baby in danger that way, but she had to make sure Aiden was all right.

"It's not Aiden," Seth warned her.

Because she was trying to fight through the panic, it took her a moment to realize what he meant. Then she spotted the movement in the trees again. Not a blur this time. Someone pushed through the low-hanging branches and staggered out into the parking lot.

Yost.

Even from the distance she could tell it was the same man who'd spoken to her in the pharmacy. He wasn't wearing a ski mask as he had been when he kidnapped her, but he did have a gun in his hand.

"Drop your weapon!" Aiden shouted to him. He came out farther from the building, his own gun aimed right at the man.

Kendall braced herself for a shoot-out. Yost had already tried to kill them at least once, and he likely wouldn't hesitate to try again.

But Yost didn't lift his weapon. It stayed by his side while he clutched his chest with his left hand.

That was when Kendall saw the blood.

The man had been shot.

"He can't die," she blurted out. "He has to tell us who hired him."

"Call an ambulance," Seth ordered the deputy. "He's alive," he added, glancing back at her. "Wait here, and I'll see what I can do to keep him that way."

Chapter Twelve

Dead.

That was not how Aiden had wanted this to play out.

He'd wanted Yost alive and talking. Especially talking. But the two gunshots to the man's chest had prevented him from saying anything, along with killing him within a matter of seconds.

Hard, though, to feel any sympathy for the man who'd kidnapped Kendall and then shot her.

Within minutes of Yost's collapsing in the parking lot, Aiden had gone after the shooter. So had two of his deputies while Seth and Jeb had stayed behind in the office to protect Kendall in case this had been some kind of diversion. But after a half-hour search of the area and no trace of Yost's killer, Aiden and the others had given up.

Yeah, definitely not how Aiden wanted this to go.

The look on Kendall's face sure wasn't helping, either. Aiden already felt as if he'd failed her and the baby, again, but now her face was even more bleached out than before, and while she was trying to put up a strong front, she was doing it by leaning on Seth.

Literally.

Aiden tried not to feel jealous about that.

After all, it was Seth who had stayed with her during

the attack, and he'd continued to stay with her after Aiden returned to the office and started the flurry of calls to arrange a full-scale search for the killer. But even after Aiden finished those calls, Kendall had stayed by Seth, his arm around her while she continued to look more and more upset.

Since Aiden had plenty to do, he ignored the arm position, tried to ignore the rest of her reactions and got back to work.

"Anything yet on the recording that I got from my mother?" he asked Jeb. The one that might implicate Joplin in all this.

The young deputy shook his head. "The Ranger Lab hasn't finished with it yet. I'm still trying to get in touch with Joplin so I can ask him about it, but he's not answering his phone. The calls are going straight to voice mail."

Not a good sign.

Well, maybe not.

The lawyer could just be tied up with another case, and if Joplin was as guilty as sin, then maybe he was already on the run. Headed far away from Kendall. And if he was indeed in flight mode, maybe he'd get caught. Aiden needed something to break in this case soon.

Also something to break that armlock Seth had on Kendall.

Yep, it was bugging him, and it was bugging him even more that he couldn't seem to stop thinking about it.

He checked out the window to see how things were progressing in the parking lot. The ME was there as Yost's body was being loaded into the van. A pair of CSIs were processing the area for evidence.

They might get lucky and find one of the spent shell casings from the killer, which would really come in handy, as the bullets that'd killed Yost had gone clean through.

If they could get their hands on just one slug or casing, they'd be able to determine the type of gun. Might even be able to get a match if the gun had been used in some other crime.

"We got the surveillance footage of the high school," Leland announced when he finished his latest call. "It's loading on my computer now, and I'll go over it frame by frame."

Good. Because all this had started near the high school, so maybe Yost's attacker had been caught on the footage.

The one good thing in all this was that no shots had been fired near the kids. That was something at least. And they'd also gotten lucky that none of the stray bullets had hit anyone in the park.

Or Kendall.

She'd been in the building during the attack, but that didn't mean she couldn't have been hurt. Her being in danger was becoming a pattern that Aiden didn't like one bit.

Of course, there were a lot of things he didn't like about their situation.

"I'm okay," Kendall said out of the blue, and that was when Aiden realized he was scowling at her. Actually, he was scowling at Seth, but she probably figured she was in on that facial expression, as well.

"Are you really?" Aiden asked. "Because the stress isn't good for you. Or the baby."

A sigh left her mouth, and she finally moved out of Seth's arms when he got a call and stepped away from her to take it. "It's not good for you, either."

She went to Aiden, sliding right into his arms as if she belonged there. "You could have been killed." Her voice was strained, barely a whisper, but he heard the emotions loud and clear.

Uh-oh.

That wasn't ordinary concern for a fellow human being. Nope. That was concern for her baby's daddy. Maybe even for him.

Aiden pulled back, looked in her eyes.

Yeah, it was concern for him all right.

After his reaction to Seth's embrace, that should have felt darn good. But it only added another layer of complications to their already complicated situation.

Kendall was pregnant with his baby. They were a Texas version of Romeo and Juliet. Star-crossed lovers. And because that story hadn't had a happy ending, this extra layer only made him worry more.

Did that make him move away from her?

Nope.

He'd clearly developed a fondness for complicated layers. Apparently, a fondness for having Kendall in his arms, too.

"I'm sorry," he whispered.

Now she looked up at him. "For what?"

"Everything" seemed like a really good answer.

Kendall stared at him, those eyes so green that they looked like spring itself. Spring with heat, of course. Even now, the heat was there. No doubt in his own eyes, too, so Aiden added another "I'm sorry" for it.

She blinked. Then the corner of her mouth lifted just a fraction.

"Next thing, you'll be apologizing for the weather." Kendall took his hand, pressed it against her stomach. "The baby and I are both fine, and you're the reason for that."

Another uh-oh.

That was playing with fire in its purest form. Her gratitude. Touching her stomach. Touching her anywhere for that matter.

Seth noticed, of course.

And Aiden didn't think it was his imagination that Mr. FBI hurried to finish his call so that he could come back to his step-aunt's aid. However, Kendall stayed put, right against Aiden, even though he did move his hand from her stomach to her shoulder.

"That was Sawyer Ryland, the agent who's investigating the attack at the jail," Seth informed them.

That got Aiden's attention. Kendall's, too. "Did he find out anything?" she asked.

"It's all preliminary stuff, but obviously plenty went wrong yesterday. Ryland thinks that a few of the male prisoners were paid off to cause a commotion to get the guards to the cell block after the power went off."

That would explain why there was only one guard at the checkpoint. "Have any of the inmates talked?"

Seth nodded. "One said money was deposited into his online account. Not much, just a couple of hundred dollars, but he's claiming the only person he dealt with is the dead guard, Deacon Lynch."

That was likely true. Because the person who'd hired Lynch and Yost probably wouldn't have wanted to have his identity revealed to inmates.

"How the heck did Lynch even become a jail guard?" Aiden asked.

Seth gave a frustrated huff. "Because he doesn't have a record as an adult. He had a juvie one, but it was sealed, of course. But what he did have was debt and plenty of it. Two ex-wives, five kids, and he was way behind in his child support payments. At least he was until a couple of days ago when he gave one of his exes the five grand he owed her."

Those debts should have been a red flag to the county agency who handled employment records for the guards, and Aiden would do some checking to see who'd dropped the ball.

But there were other things that needed checking, too.

At least five grand to Lynch alone. Probably that and maybe more to Yost and his dead co-kidnapper. The SUV, the weapons and ammo. The bill for this fiasco was adding up, and that meant a money trail.

One that Aiden had possibly already found.

"Any indication if there were other guards working with Lynch?" Kendall asked Seth before Aiden could say anything.

"None right now, but there were definitely some breaches of protocol and security during the attack. There'll be some heads rolling."

And Aiden would make sure it happened. Even though he wasn't in charge of the jail, it was right there, practically under his nose, and he didn't want anything like this happening again.

"What about the generator?" Aiden asked. "Anything back on why it failed to kick in when the power was cut?"

"Someone tampered with it," Seth answered. "But the person also disabled the camera out there."

That likely had been Lynch's doing, too. He could have managed to tamper with it hours or even days before the attack. And that led Aiden to another question he had about all this.

How had Lynch known that Kendall would be at the jail that day?

Aiden already knew that Kendall visited Jewell two to three times a week, so maybe Lynch just figured she'd be there eventually.

Or maybe it was more than that.

Maybe Lynch knew Kendall would be arriving soon to tell Jewell about the pregnancy.

Of course, that led to yet another set of questions. One in particular that Aiden needed answered.

"Sarah," Aiden said to his deputy, "could you take over looking at those surveillance films for Leland? I need to borrow him for a while."

She nodded and went to Leland's desk, not even asking why the shift in duties. Good thing, too. Aiden really didn't want to explain this to a lot of people. Seth included. But Seth latched on to it like a dog with a juicy bone.

"What's wrong?" Seth asked.

This seemed like a good time to take this conversation into Aiden's office, and he motioned for them to head there. Seth followed, of course, and Aiden wanted to come up with a reason to exclude him. One that didn't sound petty, since Seth had no doubt noticed Aiden's reaction to the arm contact with Kendall.

But the truth was, Seth might be able to help.

"For starters," Aiden said when the four of them were in his office. He aimed the intro at Seth. "You're not to go off running with what I'm about to tell you. We just need some information right now, and if it pans out, then the running can start. Got that?"

"What kind of information?" There was plenty of suspicion in Seth's voice. He didn't answer Aiden's *got that*, either.

"Money trails. I figure you can use your FBI channels to find a trail faster than I can." Aiden waited until Seth nodded. "This whole operation would have taken some money. We need to look at Joplin and Palmer to see if they've recently moved around this kind of cash."

Aiden stopped and looked at Kendall. Unlike Seth, she wasn't glaring at him. There was a healthy dose of sympathy in her eyes. It was sad, but he actually needed it. Because he was about to throw Carla under the bus.

"You'll also need to look at my mother," Aiden said to Seth.

Clearly, neither Seth nor Leland had seen that coming, so Aiden spelled it out for them. "It's possible that Carla withdrew fifty thousand from an account that she's kept hidden from the family. At best, the timing is suspicious."

Aiden didn't fill in the *at worst* part. Judging from Seth's profanity, he'd already figured it out.

"Your mother came after Kendall because of the baby?" Seth didn't wait for an answer. He cursed, turned, groaned and then turned back around.

Aiden figured Seth wanted to punch his lights out. With reason. And it wouldn't help if he told Seth that he hadn't seen it coming. A massive understatement. He hadn't wanted to believe his mother was capable of such things.

Still didn't.

"You might have to dig deep to find this account," Aiden added. "She's already aware that someone could be onto her." Best to leave his sister Shelby out of this for now. "So Carla could have closed the account."

"If it existed, I'll find it," Seth snarled.

It sounded like a threat. Which in this case was good. Because if it came down to an *at worst* conclusion, then Aiden wanted his mother behind bars. No way could he ever forgive her for trying to hurt Kendall and the baby.

Now, with that painful chore done, Aiden looked at Leland. "I want you to call my mother and tell her she's coming in for questioning. You'll need to ask her about Kendall's kidnapping, the attack at the jail. And the two murders," he added. It wasn't easy, but he got out the words.

Leland stared at him a moment and looked mighty uncomfortable. "You're sure?"

Aiden nodded. "It's got to be done. I want it official, on record. Tell her to bring her lawyer with her."

Leland stared at him, belted out some profanity. "Well, that oughta be fun," he grumbled.

"Sorry, I'd do it myself…"

"But it'd be a big-time conflict of interest," Leland finished for him. "I understand."

Aiden figured his mother wouldn't be so generous with the understanding. She'd pitch a fit, cry and disown him.

"I'm sorry," Kendall whispered to him.

That didn't make things peachy, but it did help.

More than it should have.

"I'll get started on this," Seth said, taking out his phone. He stepped out into the hall, but he'd barely gotten started when Aiden heard the footsteps.

Because every nerve in his body was on edge, Aiden automatically moved Kendall behind him. But it wasn't a threat. It was Sarah.

"I think I found something, boss," she said, her voice high-pitched and edgy. "You need to see this."

Oh, man. He had no idea what Sarah wanted to show them, but her body language said they were in for yet another round of bad news.

Sarah led him to the computer where the footage from the high school had been loaded, and the moment Aiden's attention landed on the screen, he spotted Yost.

Alive and waiting beneath a shade tree.

Yost wasn't exactly in camera range, but Sarah had blown up the shot. The result was a grainy image but enough for Aiden to tell that the man was almost certainly carrying a concealed weapon beneath his windbreaker.

"He's talking on the phone to someone here," Sarah said, scrolling through the images.

"Probably to Aiden," Kendall provided. "He called twice."

Sarah nodded. "That makes sense, because here he is again on the phone." She moved to that shot.

"Did he call anyone else?" Aiden asked the deputy.

"No. At least not while he was in camera range. Now, here's what I want you to see."

Aiden watched as Yost was on the phone, and suddenly the man's gaze rifled to the area to his right. Not in camera range.

I gotta go, Yost had said. *I see somebody.*

Whoever or whatever it was the man had seen, it'd spooked him. Yost took off running, and it didn't take long for the camera to lose him.

"Just wait," Sarah said, advancing through more of the frames.

Aiden moved closer to the screen, waiting. Hoping this wasn't something that would feel like a punch to the gut. And it didn't take long for the camera to pick up more movement.

A person, more blur than image, on the far side of the screen.

"I enhanced it," Sarah continued.

When the next image popped up, Kendall gasped and landed in Aiden's arms again. Not his mother as he'd braced himself for. But definitely one of their suspects.

Joplin was there, and he was holding a gun.

Chapter Thirteen

"You need to eat," Aiden reminded her again.

Kendall knew he was right, but she also knew her stomach was protesting the ham-and-cheese sandwich and three small containers of milk that Aiden had ordered for her from the café up the street. Apparently, Aiden had remembered that pregnant women should drink milk.

And rest.

Because he was making sure she did that, too.

He had her sitting at his desk while he munched on his own sandwich and pored over the preliminary financial info that Seth had managed to gather. Considering that it'd been only several hours since Aiden told him about Carla's withdrawal, Kendall's step-nephew had managed to come up with a lot.

Including a bank account in Carla's name that had been closed within the past twenty-four hours.

Judging from the bits and pieces of the conversation Kendall had overheard, Seth hadn't been able to find out what had been in the account, but he was still working on it.

Just as Aiden was working on making sure his mother came in for questioning.

Because Leland had initially been the one to call Carla,

Kendall hadn't heard any of that conversation, but Leland had relayed to Aiden that Carla refused, saying she didn't feel well enough to be questioned. Aiden had intervened then with yet another call that Kendall hadn't heard. However, at the end of the call, Aiden had assured Leland that Carla would be coming in at two o'clock and would be bringing her lawyer with her.

That was only an hour from now.

"Are you okay?" she asked Aiden.

He looked up from the computer screen, practically doing a double take when he saw her. It instantly made her aware of just how thrown together and frazzled she must look.

"Despite how bad I look, I feel fine," Kendall volunteered. She didn't want Aiden to worry about anything else. He already had enough.

"You don't look bad," he said, and tore his gaze from her and went back to the computer screen.

That shouldn't have made her feel even marginally better, but it did. Because for just a second, she'd seen the attraction that had gotten them where they were now.

"Seth said you used to come up with baby names," Aiden remarked, still not making eye contact with her.

That stopped Kendall in mid-sip of her milk. "He said what? When?"

"Right before he left, he pulled me aside and told me he once saw you doodling baby names. *Our* babies' names." A muscle flickered in his jaw.

That brought her to her feet. "Seth told you that?" He was a dead man, or at least a hurting one. "I was a teenager, barely thirteen, and had very romantic notions about that first kiss we'd shared."

"Yeah," Aiden agreed several snail-crawling moments

later. "Since it was my first real kiss, I had a few notions about it, too. None involved baby names, though."

"Because you're a guy." She hoped that was all there was to it anyway, and that the kiss for him had been fueled only by teenage lust.

Of course, maybe that was all it'd been, period.

And this was getting her mind off the question she really needed to ask.

"Why the devil would Seth tell you that?" she snapped.

"It was tacked onto a threat," Aiden admitted. "He said if I hurt you he'll pound me to dust."

Oh.

"Seth shouldn't have said that." She could feel the heat rise in her cheeks and sank back down into the chair.

"So, do you remember what names you doodled?" Aiden asked. "They might come in handy."

Of course she remembered. When you doodled something a hundred or more times, it was glued in your memory. "Matthew Landon."

He made a small sound. Maybe surprise, maybe not. "Matthew, my middle name."

"Landon is Roy's middle name," she provided in a mumble.

Definitely not something Aiden would want to hear. Her, merging the Braddock and McKinnon family names. Heck, there were plenty of things she was saying, plenty of things she'd done that Aiden wouldn't want her to repeat.

"I'll bet you wish your first real kiss had been with someone else," Kendall said. "So that you'd actually want to remember it."

Aiden's eyes were already dark, and they stayed that way. "If I had a do-over on that first kiss, it'd still be with you. The only thing I'd change is that there would have been a second kiss."

Had her heart actually skipped a beat? It certainly felt like it.

The silence came. The air was suddenly so still, it felt as if everything was holding its breath. Waiting. But it wasn't Aiden or her who broke that silence, it was a knock at the door. A moment later, Leland stuck his head in.

"Joplin's here," Leland said. "He wants to know what we're planning to *discuss* with him."

That got Aiden and her standing again. Well, this was a surprise, since Joplin had been ignoring Leland's calls for hours.

Aiden, Leland and she went back into the squad room, but Joplin was already making his way to them. "Your deputy here left five messages for me. Five! Before I get a sixth, you need to tell me what's going on."

"Are you armed?" Aiden asked, not budging.

Joplin made a sound of outrage. "Yes. I have a permit to carry a concealed weapon."

"So do thousands of people, but you're not going into the room with Kendall until you've surrendered your weapon. You're a murder suspect, Joplin."

No sound of outrage this time, but the lawyer did go pale. Kendall wanted to feel sorry for him, but if he'd truly done these horrible attacks, then she wanted him behind bars for the rest of his life.

Joplin took his gun from a shoulder holster that his jacket had hidden and handed it to Aiden. Aiden tipped his head to Leland. "Frisk him."

If looks could have killed, Joplin would have done just that with the glare he shot Aiden, but he submitted to the search. Once Leland gave them the all-clear, Aiden handed his deputy Joplin's gun and then escorted the lawyer not to his office but to an interview room.

"Bring me the recording," Aiden added to Leland.

"What recording?" Joplin asked.

But Aiden didn't answer. After they were seated and Leland delivered the phone with the message, Aiden hit the play button.

"You'll get half the money now and half when the job's done," Joplin said on the recording.

"You want it done at her place?" the second man asked.

"It doesn't matter," Joplin answered. *"Just get it done."*

Joplin was cursing before the recording even finished. "How the hell did you get that?"

"It doesn't matter. What I want to know—is it true? Did you hire those men to kidnap Kendall?"

"No!" Joplin yelled, and he repeated the word several times. He looked at her, the glare gone. "I wouldn't hurt you, Kendall. You know that."

She wanted to believe it. "I'm not sure of a lot of things right now."

That brought on more profanity. "You did this," he accused Aiden. "You turned her against me."

"Unless you can explain that tape, Kendall won't need anyone to turn her against you." Aiden leaned in and got right in Joplin's face. "Did you hire those thugs?"

"No." This time when Joplin answered, it wasn't a shout, but it was just as intense, and his eyes had narrowed to slits. "The man on that recording with me is Barry McNease. He does occasional legwork for me during investigations."

"What kind of legwork?" Aiden pressed.

Joplin stayed quiet for several seconds. "It's no secret that I believe Jewell is innocent, so I've been looking at other possible suspects. Something that the cops and DA didn't do."

"Oh, they looked," Aiden argued. "But everything pointed to Jewell. Sorry," he added, glancing at Kendall.

She waved him off because he was right. Everything did indeed point to Jewell.

"Was this McNease helping you look for suspects?" Kendall asked.

Joplin nodded. "I wanted surveillance cameras set up so I could keep tabs on Meredith Bellows. She was someone else who was rumored to have had an affair with Whitt shortly before he was murdered."

It wasn't the first time Meredith's name had come up, but the woman had been dismissed as a suspect. There hadn't even been any solid corroboration of her affair with Whitt. Just rumors and gossip.

"Meredith had an alibi," Kendall reminded him.

"She did, but her husband's alibi was thin at best. I think he could have killed Whitt, and he's big enough to have disposed of the body himself."

Aiden dragged in a long, weary breath. "Did you ask Sheriff McKinnon to question Mr. Bellows?"

"Yes, and he did, but Bellows denied everything, of course. I thought maybe if I watched them, the Bellowses would do something that I could use to get the charges dismissed against Jewell."

Kendall went back over every word of the recording. Yes, it was possible that that's what Joplin was doing, but he was acting pretty suspicious for an innocent man.

"Let me guess," Aiden said, "these cameras weren't going in a public place. And you had no authorization for them."

Bingo. That would explain the guilty look.

Maybe.

"Since you're a lawyer," Aiden went on, "I don't have to tell you that anything you obtained from those cameras couldn't have been used in a court of law."

"It's the same for that recording," Joplin fired back.

"But I wasn't looking to use the footage to convict Meredith or her husband. I was looking for anything that I could turn into an investigation to help Jewell."

That was really grasping at straws, but then again the trial wasn't that far off, and everyone on both sides was feeling anxious and desperate.

Kendall included.

Aiden got in Joplin's face again. "Now tell me why you're on a surveillance video near the high school shortly before a man was shot and killed."

For just a moment, Joplin's eyes widened in surprise, and then he frantically shook his head. "No, you're not going to try to pin that on me—"

"Why were you there?" Aiden demanded, talking right over Joplin.

"Because I got a call from one of the PIs I'd hired, and he asked me to meet him there."

Kendall stared at him. "Really?"

"Really!" Joplin snapped. "I didn't speak to the PI himself but rather someone from his office. When I arrived, he wasn't there, and I saw that suspicious-looking guy hanging around, so I drew my gun."

She wanted to groan. It was so unlikely that it made it likely. And while he looked guilty, Joplin could indeed have been set up.

"I'm trying to clear Jewell," Joplin restated. "I don't need to kill anyone to do that."

Aiden did groan. Obviously, this was as frustrating for him as it was for her. "If you're so innocent, then why did you ignore the five calls from my deputy?" Aiden continued.

Kendall was interested in hearing the answer to that as well, but before Joplin could respond, the door flew open.

One look at Leland's face, and Kendall knew something was wrong, again.

Apparently, so did Aiden, because he cursed. "What happened now?"

"Palmer and your mother got into an argument outside city hall." Leland swallowed hard. "Carla's holding him at gunpoint."

THIS DAY JUST kept going downhill.

Aiden had hoped Leland was wrong, that Carla truly wasn't involved in a mess that she shouldn't be involved in. Yet there she was, standing on the sidewalk outside the courthouse.

And yeah, she had her .38 revolver aimed right at Palmer.

"Oh, God." Kendall's gaze went to the fiasco about fifteen yards ahead of them.

Some divine intervention might help right now, but Aiden figured he'd be the one to handle this.

"Stay down," Aiden warned her for the umpteenth time. "And wait with Kendall," he ordered Leland.

That put a frustrated look on Leland's face, probably because he wanted to be out there with Aiden, but the deputy was staying put with Kendall. There'd be no arguments about that. It'd been bad enough that he'd had to bring her here, but Aiden hadn't wanted to leave her in the building with Joplin.

Of course, he also didn't want Kendall anywhere near gunfire, either, so that was why he'd come in a squad car. Aiden fully intended to disarm his mother immediately, but just in case somebody else started shooting, he wanted Kendall protected as much as possible.

"Be careful," Kendall said when he opened the cruiser door to get out. Her expression was similar to Leland's but a lot more intense.

"It's my mother," Aiden reminded her. "She won't shoot me."

He hoped.

But since that didn't lessen the worried look on Kendall's face, he brushed a kiss on her cheek. Then her mouth.

Oh, man.

He was in a lot of trouble, and it didn't have anything to do with what he was about to face. Soon, very soon, Kendall and he were going to have to sit down and talk about what the heck was going on between them. And also start making plans for the baby. Plans that would have to wait until he put out yet another fire.

Kendall added a second "be careful" as Aiden got out and started toward Palmer and his mother. They'd drawn a crowd, at least a dozen people who were thankfully hovered behind the building and nearby cars.

"Stay back," Aiden warned everyone. "And put down that gun!" He added some volume and grit to his voice for that last order to Carla.

His mother spared him a glance but didn't lower her weapon. Though she was licensed to carry the gun, he wasn't even sure if she could shoot straight with it. And Aiden didn't want to find out.

Everything about Carla's body was wired and stiff. Unlike Palmer. His hands were raised in the air, but there wasn't much concern on his face. This was like a joke to him, but Aiden sure wasn't laughing.

"Aiden," the man greeted as if this were a friendly meeting. "Glad you got here so fast. Your mother's clearly lost her mind."

"I've found it," Carla snapped. "And I know Palmer's the one who's trying to set me up."

"Set you up?" Aiden asked, going closer. He didn't

want to lunge for the gun, since it might accidentally go off, but he had to get it out of her hands.

"For Kendall's kidnapping." Carla sucked in her breath, making a hiccuping sound. And there were tears on her cheeks.

A gun and tears were never a good combination.

"Just why would I set you up?" Palmer asked. Butter wouldn't melt in that mouth.

Aiden could think of a reason or two for a setup, but his mother voiced it first. "Because you hate me and my family. Because you'd like to see Whitt's killer walk. Because you're on the side of the McKinnons."

Palmer shrugged. "That doesn't mean I'd obstruct justice to get those things."

Yes, it did, but there wasn't any proof of it—yet—and even if there had been, the more immediate concern was disarming Carla.

"Hand me the gun, Mom," Aiden demanded.

Carla's hand started to shake. More tears came. But she lowered the gun, then gave it to him.

The safety was on, Aiden noticed right off. Maybe that meant she hadn't planned on doing bodily harm after all.

"The rest of you can clear out," Aiden said to the bystanders. "The three of us are talking," he added to Palmer and Carla.

Normally, Aiden would already have taken this chat back to his office, but he really didn't want to cram Palmer and his mother into the cruiser with Kendall. Of course, they'd eventually have to be brought in to make a statement and in his mother's case, an arrest, so he motioned for Leland. When his deputy stepped out of the cruiser, Aiden instructed him to call Sarah to come to the scene so she could escort Carla to the station.

His mother wiped at the tears that just kept coming.

Aiden fished out his handkerchief, handed it to her and looked at Palmer, hoping the man would get started with an explanation about this that would make some sense.

"Your mother accused me of setting up some kind of bank account in her name," Palmer said. "An account that supposedly someone used to hire those men who kidnapped Kendall."

Interesting. "Did you?" he asked Palmer.

"Of course not. Why would I?"

"For all those reasons Carla just mentioned," Aiden pointed out.

Palmer cocked his head to the side. "Really? If I'd wanted to get back at Carla, I could think of a better way."

Since that sounded like a threat, Aiden mimicked his cocky head tilt. "What way?"

"One that wouldn't involve hurting Kendall," Palmer said.

"Yet you think I'd do something to hurt my own son?" Carla snarled.

Palmer shrugged again. "Maybe that wasn't your plan. Maybe you thought you could get Kendall arrested and jailed for a long time for setting up her own kidnapping and destroying evidence. Then you could raise the Braddock baby she's carrying. All without putting your son in danger."

Too bad it was indeed the kind of plan a sick mind could come up with. A mind filled with hate and the need for revenge.

Like his mother's.

But Palmer's mind was equally sick.

From the corner of his eye, Aiden saw Sarah pull up in a patrol car, so he motioned for Carla and Palmer to follow him. Leland got out of the cruiser. So did Kendall.

"I know Palmer set up that account," Carla mumbled.

"You have proof?" Aiden asked.

"No," she admitted after several long moments.

"Because there is no proof," Palmer argued. "If I'd wanted to set her up, I wouldn't have used a bank account. It leaves too many trails. I would have just hired some lowlifes and told them they were working for Carla. Then I would have arranged for them to go to the cops with that news."

True. Bank accounts were messy. And there had indeed been such an account, as Shelby had seen it. So why would his mother risk that?

"I'm betting Carla probably didn't think a bank account leaves all kinds of telltale signs, even when it's erased. Follow the money trail," Palmer insisted, pointing his finger at Aiden. "It'll lead to your mother."

Carla spun around and would have launched herself at Palmer if Aiden hadn't grabbed her. Palmer laughed. And Kendall got there in time to step between Aiden and the idiot that Aiden wanted to punch. He wouldn't have done it, of course, but he sure wanted to wipe that smirk off Palmer's face.

"I told you Carla was crazy," Palmer went on. "She needs to be locked away in the loony bin *again*."

Aiden froze. So did Carla. And Palmer got that gleam in his eye.

"You didn't know." Palmer didn't laugh, but it was close enough. "Tell him, Carla, or I will."

Oh, man.

Aiden was a thousand percent sure he wasn't going to like this.

He especially didn't like it when Palmer's gaze shifted to Kendall. "Or maybe it'd be better if Aiden heard it from you."

Kendall didn't answer, though Aiden was certain she knew what Palmer was talking about.

"I was in an institution," Carla muttered. "It happened a long time ago, before I even married your father."

Judging from the way Kendall dodged Aiden's gaze, she knew something more about this than she'd already told him.

"Does this have anything to do with the elderly woman you were telling me about?" Aiden asked her.

She nodded, eventually. "After I pressed Jewell for anything I could use to help her, she gave me the name of the psychiatrist that Carla saw all those years ago. He's long been dead, but I tracked down the nurse who worked for him." Kendall's voice was as ragged as his mother's. "But I didn't know that your mother had actually been in the institution."

Kendall's comment put some flames in Carla's eyes. "Whitt must have told Jewell about the psychiatrist," Carla said.

"Why were you in an institution?" Aiden demanded.

More flames popped into her eyes, directed at both Palmer and Kendall. She aimed something considerably worse at Aiden.

"I'm not saying another word until I speak to my lawyer," Carla snapped. And she stormed off toward Sarah, getting into the cruiser with the deputy.

Even though Aiden wanted answers, he didn't go after her. He also didn't leave Kendall standing out in the open any longer. He hurried her back to the car with Leland, but the moment they were inside, Aiden snapped toward her.

"Start talking," he demanded. "And, Leland, get us back to the office."

Leland pulled away from the building, but Kendall sure didn't start talking. It seemed to take her several moments just to gather her breath. Or maybe she was trying to figure out the best spin she could put on this. However, there was no good spin to something she'd obviously kept from him.

"I wasn't even sure it was true," she finally started. "Whitt told Jewell that Carla had needed psychiatric help when she was a teenager."

Not exactly ideal pillow talk, spilling secrets about your wife to your lover. "Why was Carla there? And why am I just now hearing about this after all these years?"

Kendall shook her head. "There are no records of it. I know because I looked for them."

Yes, so that Kendall could try to pin his father's murder on anyone but her precious sister. Aiden tried not to be riled to the core about that, but it was hard to do.

"Tell me everything that Whitt told Jewell," he demanded. "And everything the nurse told you."

Another nod, followed by another long pause. "I didn't get much of anything from the nurse, just a confirmation that the doctor she worked for had treated your mother. No details."

Aiden studied her expression. "But Jewell got some details from Whitt, didn't she?"

"Details that Jewell wasn't even sure were true," Kendall added.

He stared at her. "Details that I want to hear right now."

Kendall swallowed hard. Nodded. "According to what Whitt told Jewell, your mother tried to murder someone."

Chapter Fourteen

Aiden was pacing across his office while he talked on the phone, something he'd been doing for at least an hour since they had arrived back at the station.

For this latest call, he hadn't put the phone on speaker, so Kendall could only guess what was going on. Of course, she didn't need to hear the other half of the conversation to know that things weren't going well. Aiden was scowling. The muscles in his face were tight. And he had a crushing grip on the phone.

Kendall knew he was talking yet again to his sister Shelby, but she had no idea how much longer this particular call would go on. Probably until Aiden got the information he wanted.

Information he hadn't gotten from Carla.

His mother was sitting in an interview room, waiting for her lawyer to show up, and she'd made it crystal clear that she wasn't talking to her son or his deputy. Of course, she hadn't talked to Kendall, either, though she had glared at her every chance she got. Kendall tried not to glare back, but it was hard. After all, Carla might be responsible for the kidnapping and the attacks, and if so, that meant Aiden's mom had put the baby in serious danger.

If Carla had truly done that, Kendall would never forgive her.

However, the jury was still out on the woman's guilt.

It would take time to prove if she had any involvement with the kidnappers. She would be charged for the altercation with Palmer, of course, and endangering the public, but as there'd been no shots fired, Kendall was betting the woman would be released on bail.

"What else haven't you told me?" Aiden growled to his sister. A question he would no doubt repeat to Kendall once he had the chance.

Again, she couldn't hear Shelby's answer, but despite his obvious anger, Aiden motioned for Kendall to eat. It was yet another meal he'd had delivered from the café. This time a pasta salad and more milk. Because she didn't want to add to his misery, Kendall nibbled at it.

Aiden's conversation went on with his sister for at least another minute before he snarled, "Don't you dare withhold anything else." And he jabbed the end call button with far more force than necessary.

Before turning to her.

He didn't glare at her, not exactly. But it was close enough. Then he groaned and cursed.

Kendall decided it was best if she just got this out in the open.

"I didn't know your mother had actually been in an institution. I swear. Jewell never said. Heck, she probably doesn't even know. We only knew that Carla had seen a psychiatrist." Kendall paused. "But Shelby knew?"

He nodded, eventually. Cursed some more.

"How did she find out?" Kendall asked. "Because I tried, and every call, email and question was nothing but a roadblock."

"Shelby's a little too good at getting past roadblocks," he mumbled.

Probably because she was an investigative reporter

and had plenty of connections. Or maybe Carla had even told her.

"My mother wasn't raised around here," Aiden said, dropping down in the chair across from her. "That's why no one knew. Well, no one except for my father and her folks, who've now passed away. As you said, the records no longer exist, but Shelby managed to track down some employees who worked at the facility."

Kendall didn't press with another question. She just waited until Aiden was ready to continue.

"When she was eighteen, Carla apparently met Lee Palmer," Aiden finally went on. "He was twenty, a broke rodeo rider, and he was engaged to a very wealthy woman. Carla's family had money, too, so they ran in the same social circles as Palmer's fiancée. Depending on whose side you believe, Carla had an affair with Palmer. Or else she became obsessed with him and wanted him to break off the engagement. When he didn't do that, she tried to run him over with her car."

"Sweet heaven." Kendall was glad she was sitting down. "But why hasn't Palmer said anything about it? This would have been the perfect information to get the DA and cops to look at someone other than Jewell for your father's murder.

"Sorry," she added. That was probably something Aiden didn't need to hear her say.

Though he no doubt had already thought about it.

He waved off her apology and had a long sip of water, probably wishing it was something a lot stronger. "Shelby only has bits and pieces, but apparently Palmer agreed to drop the charges against Carla for a sealed settlement and the agreement that she'd go to the institution for help."

It all became clear. For his silence, Palmer no doubt got a boatload of money from Carla's wealthy family, and if he'd indeed had an affair with her, then the sealed settlement might have prevented his fiancée from finding out about his cheating. Also, Carla's family could have a non-disclosure clause for Palmer himself. That way, if Palmer had indeed discussed it with anybody, he could have lost the settlement money.

And that brought Kendall to consider something else.

"If Carla and Palmer had this bad history, how did they end up living so close to each other?" she asked.

"The Braddocks have lived around here for six generations. Palmer moved here not long after my parents got married."

Good grief. Palmer had no doubt used the settlement money to start his own cattle empire. Right under Carla's nose. And the bad blood had just continued with Palmer's constant presence stirring the pot.

"I'll have to tell the DA all this," Aiden grumbled.

Yes, and while it might end up helping Jewell's case, Kendall knew that Jewell wouldn't want to be helped at the expense of someone else. Not even Carla.

This was tearing Aiden apart. She could see it. Feel it. So she stood and went to him. He got up as well, and his expression had a *back off* vibe to it. Kendall ignored it and put her arms around him. Too bad her stitches brushed against his shirtsleeve, causing her to wince.

And causing Aiden to curse.

He pulled her back, lifted the bandage and had a look. There was still no relief on his face, though. "You didn't pop a stitch, but you need to be more careful."

True. So, when she reached for him a second time, she put only her unstitched right arm around him.

Their gazes met. For some very long moments. Before his gaze dropped to her mouth, a place it usually went when they were within a half mile of each other. Kendall knew, because she was looking at his mouth, too.

"You need to be more careful," he repeated.

Since they were no longer talking about stitches, Kendall eked out a smile. And kissed him. Like their other kisses, this one had all the fire, and it slid right through her. But also like with all the others, the guilt came.

Especially now.

With this news about his mother, it almost felt as if they were on different sides again. Of course, with the baby and the attraction pulling them right back together, it seemed as if they could overcome even this latest wrinkle.

Almost.

"We can't keep skirting around this," he said.

That rid her of any trace of a smile. Because he also slid his hand between them and put it over her stomach. Definitely no smiling matter.

"You want shared custody." Kendall moved away from him. "But for that to work, we'd need to live fairly close to each other. Especially when he's still a baby. That means one of us living in a place where we won't exactly be comfortable."

She was fairly sure that Aiden would want her to be that *one of us*. After all, he was grounded in place as the county sheriff, and she could live anywhere in the state. However, that was why Kendall had made plans to move—so that she wouldn't be in the middle of his family feud.

"In addition to a move *for one of us*, you'd also need a nanny," she went on. "And you'd have to make sure that your family doesn't despise the baby so much that it could be traumatic for him."

Aiden stayed quiet a moment. "You've given this some thought."

"Plenty."

"And you don't think it can work," he concluded.

Kendall huffed. "I hadn't thought it would work from the beginning. That's why I was planning to leave." Now she paused. "I guess my feelings have changed a little about that, though."

"Because we keep kissing."

Aiden certainly had a way of cutting right to the heart of the matter. Of course it was because of those kisses. Even now, it was because her body was still humming from having been in his arms.

"Nobody in my family will despise this child," he said with absolute authority. "And if they do, they won't be in my life for long."

It was the right thing to say to make her feel better. But the wrong thing to muddle her mind even more. Kendall still had no idea how they were going to fix this.

"Come on," Aiden said, taking her by the hand. "Even when my mother's lawyer shows up, I shouldn't be the one who does the interview. I'll take you back to your place so you can get some rest. Sarah can follow us."

Kendall didn't say no to that. They'd been at the sheriff's office most of the day, and it wouldn't be long before it was dark. Now that both her attackers were dead, the prison guard, too, she could breathe a little easier, but there'd be no relaxing until the person who'd hired them was behind bars.

And maybe that would soon happen.

But it probably wouldn't happen tonight unless they got a confession from Carla or one of their other suspects.

When they stepped out of Aiden's office, Kendall spotted Carla seated at one of the interview tables. Her back was board straight. Her eyes, focused on the drab gray wall.

"Leland will be doing your interview when your lawyer arrives," Aiden told his mother.

Carla's mouth tightened, though she still didn't look directly at them. Nor did she speak. Which might have been for the best. There wasn't much she could have said that would make this situation better.

Aiden got Kendall outside and in his truck, and with Sarah in a cruiser right behind them, they headed to Kendall's house in Sweetwater Springs. The place had been her home for a long time, but since the attacks, it felt more like a holding cell.

"You're probably sick of sleeping on the floor," she said. Then she winced. It sounded like an invitation for him to share the bed with her.

He smiled that half smile. The one that had no doubt seduced many women. Of course, Aiden didn't have to smile to seduce her. He did that just by breathing.

"I'm not leaving until we're sure the danger has passed," he insisted. "The floor's optional." He paused a heartbeat. Then cursed. "Except we both know that's a bad idea."

Yes, they did. Sleeping together again would just cloud their minds and get in the way of working out a custody decision. Of course, it might ease some of this tension between them.

Kendall mentally repeated that rationalization and groaned.

Oh, yes. She had a bad case of Aiden Braddock all right.

"Twenty minutes," he said when he pulled into her driveway. He checked the time on the dashboard clock. "If I move to the east side of Clay Ridge, I'd still be close enough to work, and I'd be close enough to you and the baby." He dropped a quick, unexpected kiss on her mouth. "Just give it some thought."

Kendall would. Especially since he'd included her in that and not just the baby. That kiss helped, too.

The fantasy wheel started again. Of her, Aiden and the baby being a family. Definitely not something she should have on her mind, since she'd be sharing a bedroom with Aiden again.

Sarah got out of the cruiser, waiting for them to go in, so Aiden and she hurried to the porch. Kendall unlocked the door, and she immediately turned to the keypad on the interior wall so she could disarm the security system.

But it wasn't armed.

There was no beeping sound, and the lights were off on the keypad.

"Something's wrong," Kendall whispered.

And then she heard the footsteps.

EVERYTHING SEEMED TO happen at once. The porch light blinked off, and Aiden drew his gun when he saw a blur of motion to his left.

Right behind Kendall.

She made a muffled sound of surprise, and it took Aiden a split second to realize that it was muffled because someone had grabbed her from behind and had slapped his hand over her mouth.

That someone put a gun to her head.

From what Aiden could see, it appeared to be a man wearing a ski mask, similar to the ones that the other kidnappers had used.

Hell.

This was another thug coming after Kendall again.

"What's wrong?" Sarah called out, and from the corner of his eye, Aiden saw the deputy making her way to the house.

"Tell her to stay back," the masked guy warned Aiden.

He took his hand from Kendall's mouth so he could hook his arm around her neck. "And put down your gun."

Aiden did the first, motioning for Sarah to stay put. He didn't want this moron shooting her. Didn't want him hurting Kendall, either, so that meant he had to figure out how to diffuse the situation.

Fast.

"How'd you get in here?" Kendall demanded, sounding more defiant than strong. Maybe because like Aiden, she was fed up with these attacks.

"Hacked into your security system," he said, and in the same breath he tipped his head to Aiden's gun. "I said drop it."

The last time Aiden had refused to do that, Kendall had been shot in the arm. Still, if he didn't have a weapon, there was nothing to stop this guy from just shooting him and taking off with Kendall.

"What do you want?" Aiden snapped.

"To take her out of this house. Soon, someone will contact you about what you need to do to get her back."

So this was indeed another kidnapping attempt. Probably another attempt at getting him to obstruct justice or destroy evidence.

Or to make it look that way.

"Just do as you're told," the man added, "and Miss O'Neal will be okay."

Kendall shook her head a little, obviously not believing him. Aiden wasn't buying it, either. But there was something about this situation that told him loads. If the guy had wanted to shoot Aiden, he could have already done it. He could have pulled the trigger the moment that Aiden stepped inside.

So why hadn't he?

Why hadn't this guy taken out the biggest threat—the

county sheriff? That was an unsettling thought because it led him back to his mother.

Aiden pushed that aside, since it wouldn't help him now, and he tried to figure out the best way to approach this. The guy had the gun to Kendall's head, but Aiden had to believe the kidnapper had been told to bring her in alive. That meant he didn't want to kill her.

Well, not now anyway.

"Come on," the guy said to Kendall. He dropped his left arm to her waist and started dragging her out of the entry.

Unlike the other kidnapping thugs, this guy was a little shaky. And he'd apparently given up on his demand to disarm Aiden. That could be both good and bad. Good because a nervous kidnapper would be more likely to make a mistake. Bad because a mistake could lead to Kendall getting hurt.

Aiden motioned for Sarah to come closer, and he waited for the guy to glance behind him to see where he was about to step.

That was the best chance Aiden figured he'd get.

Aiden tossed his gun aside, figuring he'd need both hands for this half-thought-out plan. He did. Aiden pushed Kendall to the side, praying that she wouldn't fall, and in the same motion, he went after the goon. He put his old football skills to work and tackled the guy.

They both went to the floor.

His shoulder hit, hard. So hard that the pain shot through him. Aiden hoped he hadn't dislocated it, because the guy tried to wallop him upside the head with his gun. Aiden grabbed hold of the guy's shooting wrist to stop him from doing that and from getting off a shot.

Kendall scrambled out of the way, thank God. At least Aiden thought that was what she was doing, but she didn't run out of the house and toward Sarah. She scooped up his gun and tried to take aim at the would-be kidnapper.

"Run!" Aiden managed to shout to her.

She didn't listen. Worse, she didn't get behind Sarah when the deputy made it into the house. Sarah, too, took aim. Not that she had any more of a clean shot than Kendall did. Aiden and the masked idiot were punching each other's lights out, too close to each other for Sarah or Kendall to try to take out the kidnapper.

Using as much force as he could, Aiden bashed the guy's shooting hand against the marble floor. It didn't work. The guy held on. So Aiden did it again.

And again.

Aiden could have sworn that he heard fingers breaking, and finally the idiot let go. The gun dropped from his hand. But before Aiden could even knock it out of the way, the guy scooped it up again and took aim.

At Kendall.

The blast was deafening, and it echoed through the nearly empty house. Echoed through Aiden, too, and even though he couldn't actually hear, he yelled out Kendall's name. He turned, praying that she hadn't been shot again. But she was standing there.

Aiden said a quick prayer of thanks for that.

But she still had his gun in her hand. A gun that was still aimed at the kidnapper. Unlike Kendall and Sarah, the man wasn't standing. He'd flopped back onto the floor, his breath rattling in his throat.

"I shot him," Kendall said, and sounded as if she was about to fall on the floor, too. Not from an injury but from the shock of what'd just happened.

She had indeed shot the man.

"Call an ambulance," Aiden told Sarah.

He scrambled across the floor, tore off the man's mask.

A stranger. A stranger who was about to bleed out. No way would he last long enough for the medics to get there.

"Who hired you?" Aiden demanded. "Tell me!"

But the man didn't speak. His eyelids drifted down, and there was another gravelly breath.

His last one.

Kendall made a sound, too. One that let Aiden know that she was within seconds of falling apart. He made it to her in one step and pulled her into his arms.

Chapter Fifteen

Kendall was afraid if she stopped moving, she would collapse. First, she'd paced while waiting for the ME and Jeb, the young deputy, to arrive. Of course, Aiden had tried to get her to sit down, but she couldn't. She had to keep moving. It was the only thing that seemed to be keeping the horrible images at bay.

She could still feel the gun in her hand even though Aiden had long since taken it from her. She could also still hear the sound of the blast. Could still see the glimpses of the kidnapper falling to the floor. The pacing pushed them aside, for several seconds anyway, but it was that brief reprieve that was keeping her from falling apart.

"You ready?" Aiden asked Sarah, and the deputy nodded. "Let's go," he said then to Kendall.

He led her out of the house, past the group of CSIs and lawmen who'd come to investigate the shooting, and they headed to his truck. Sarah was right behind them and got into one of the cruisers.

By Kendall's calculations, it'd been nearly an hour since the shooting, and a death almost certainly meant Aiden and Sarah had plenty of work to do. But he didn't drive toward his office.

"Are we going to your place?" she asked.

"Yeah." He glanced around, no doubt to make sure there wasn't another attacker lurking around. "Sorry that it'll have some bad memories for you, but it was either there or a hotel. At least my house has a security system. And this time, I'll use it."

That brought on the images again, and even though she didn't say a word, Aiden reached over, took her hand and brushed a kiss on her knuckles.

"This wasn't your fault," he said, his voice strained but yet soothing at the same time. "You did what you had to do."

"I didn't intend to kill him. I only wanted to stop him from shooting. Now he can't say who hired him to come after us."

"You," Aiden corrected. "Not us."

Because her head was a mess, it took Kendall a moment to realize what he meant. The kidnapper had definitely come after her, and he'd been trying to get her out of her house and to heaven knew where when he was dragging her out of the foyer. And then there was what he'd said to Aiden.

Soon, someone will contact you about what you need to do to get her back.

"Someone still wants to use me to get you to destroy evidence," Kendall concluded.

"Or maybe that someone wants it to appear that way." He drew in a long, weary breath. "Whoever hired this latest thug could just want you dead. Maybe because he or she believes Yost said something in the pharmacy that could blow his boss's identity."

"But Yost didn't say anything that could have done that."

Had he?

Like now, she'd certainly had a lot on her mind, so Yost could have accidentally revealed something.

But what?

"If there's anything to remember about what he said, it'll come to you," Aiden added.

Maybe. But if she did remember, would it be in time to stop them from being attacked again?

"I need to press all three suspects once more," Aiden went on. "Well, at least the two who might talk. My mother's lawyer told her to remain silent."

Something normally reserved for the guilty. But there probably wasn't much that Carla could say that would make her look innocent. Not about the fifty grand or her stay in the institution. A past stay in an institution wasn't proof of guilt, but the DA could argue that she had a history of violent behavior. Of course, the DA would need more than just a history to file charges against her for these kidnapping attempts and attacks.

"Anything on Palmer's and Joplin's financials?" she asked.

Kendall wasn't even sure she wanted to have this conversation, but it was better than just sitting there and staring out at the darkness. Plus, her hands had started to tremble again. And Aiden noticed all right, because he was still holding on to one of them.

"Nothing so far," he answered, "but that doesn't mean we won't find something. Eventually, this person has to make a mistake."

Yes, but that didn't mean he or she couldn't keep hiring gunmen.

Aiden took the turn to his small ranch, and when he reached the house, he stopped the truck directly in front of the porch. Definitely some bad memories here, since it was where she'd been shot and one of the kidnappers had died.

Of course, her own house was loaded with plenty of bad memories now, too. Along with the jail and the sheriff's office. She was running out of places where she felt safe.

They waited until Sarah had parked, and Aiden hurried them inside. This time, he set the security system and had Sarah and her stay in the entry while he did a thorough search of the house. No doubt to make sure someone hadn't broken in and was lurking inside, waiting to attack.

There was no sign that it'd been a crime scene just forty-eight hours earlier. Someone had even cleaned up the blood on the floor. Kendall was especially thankful for that.

"There's the guest bedroom and a bath next to it," Aiden said to Sarah, pointing to a room just off the hall. "Help yourself to whatever's in the fridge. I'll have Kendall upstairs with me."

Upstairs, in his bedroom.

Despite the fact that it meant another night in close quarters with Aiden, at least the second floor would be a little more secure, since an attacker would have to get past Sarah and then up the stairs. Plus, with the security system, they should have enough warning.

She hoped.

"I'll have someone pick you up clothes and such in the morning," he told her while he shucked off his holster.

When they got to his room, he dropped the holster on the nightstand and was about to sit down on the bed when he looked at her, then at the floor. Aiden didn't groan, not out loud anyway, but she could see the dread of spending another night on the floor.

Kendall was dreading it, too.

For a different reason.

She was still trembling, her mind and body a basket case, but Kendall knew there was a fix for that. A temporary one anyway.

And the fix was Aiden.

"Yes, I'm sure of this," she said because she knew the question would come up fast.

Heck, it still might come up, but Kendall did something about that, too. She slipped her arm around Aiden's neck, pulled him to her and kissed him.

AIDEN KNEW THIS was a mistake, but he just didn't care.

He was tired of fending off this fire. Tired of wanting and not having. And especially tired of not having Kendall in his arms.

Well, he had her there now.

A sane man would have just kissed her a time or two and put her to bed. *Alone.* So that she could get the sleep she needed. But because he'd been forced to kill a man a time or two and knew what was going on in her head, there wouldn't be much sleep for her tonight.

Kendall made a soft sound, part relief, part pleasure. Aiden was right there with her on that. Yeah, kissing her amped up every part of his body. Made him burn. But there was also the buzz beneath the fire. The feeling that this should already have happened again.

Multiple times.

He pulled her closer, mindful of the stitches in her arm, but if they were bothering her in the least, she didn't show it. However, what she did show was that she was just as eager to keep up the kisses as he was. So Aiden moved his mouth to her neck, dropping some more kisses along the way.

Kendall responded with another of those silky sounds.

Not much relief in it this time, though. The heat was taking over and making them both crazier than they already were.

Somehow in all that craziness, Aiden remembered to lock the door just in case Sarah came up to check on them. He also killed the lights and kept Kendall away from the window. Once he had those things taken care of, he went back to kissing her the way he wanted.

All over her body.

From her neck, he went to her breasts, shoving up her top so there'd be no clothes in the way. He wanted his mouth on her bare skin, and that was exactly what he got.

She tasted like everything good that he'd ever wanted or needed.

Probably not a good thing, but he was past the point of reason here. Past the point of anything that didn't involve getting Kendall on that bed.

Kendall wasn't exactly fighting the idea, either. She was already battling with his shirt, trying to get the buttons undone while she surrendered to the kisses that'd made their way down to her belly. Going with his no-clothes rule, Aiden rid her of her jeans. Then her panties.

And he kissed her in another spot that he'd wanted to kiss since this insanity started.

Oh, yes. This was definitely leading straight to the bed.

Kendall got them moving in that direction all on her own. While she yanked at his clothes. While she cursed him, too, but Aiden was pretty sure it was the good kind of cursing brought on by the need for immediate relief of this fire inside them. He knew exactly how she felt.

They landed on the bed, Aiden adjusting her at the last second so that her arm wouldn't be pressed against him or the mattress. But her stitches seemed to be the last thing on Kendall's mind.

Ditto for the pregnancy.

That stopped him for a moment because he darn sure should have considered it before now.

"Is this okay?" Aiden glanced down at her stomach.

"Of course." And she hauled him right back to her, along with ridding him of the rest of his clothes.

Aiden accepted her *of course*. Obviously, at this point he would have accepted almost anything as long as he could have her.

His bare skin against hers only revved up the heat. And soon, very soon, Aiden knew that foreplay was about to go right out the window. Later, if there was a later that involved kisses and such, maybe he could make it up to her. For now, though, he just took everything Kendall offered him.

Everything.

He adjusted their positions again, moving on top of her, and eased into her. He immediately felt that punch of need explode in his head. It was something he would have liked to have savored for a while, but Aiden knew that wasn't going to happen.

That need dictated everything. The speed and intensity. And it wasn't just for him but for Kendall, too.

"Let's finish this," she said in that satin voice that he couldn't have resisted even if she hadn't been looking up at him.

Aiden kissed her. Because it was his way of holding on to this. With the taste of her on his mouth. The heat of her skin on his.

With everything falling right into place, Aiden finished this.

Chapter Sixteen

Kendall nearly jumped when she opened her eyes. It was dark, everything unfamiliar around her. Well, everything except for the man next to her.

Aiden.

She was in his bed, in his house, and hours earlier they'd had incredible sex. This time without having been the least bit drunk. He'd regret it, of course. Heck, she might, too, but for now she just settled down and enjoyed the moment and the view.

And what a view it was.

Aiden was on his stomach. Completely naked. And the moonlight was streaming in through the window, spilling like a spotlight over his perfect body. He'd always been hot, even when they were teenagers, and now he was many steps past the hot stage.

Of course, looking at him only reminded her of how much she wanted him all over again. And how much that want for him complicated their lives. A custody arrangement would be difficult enough without them lusting after each other, and she figured this attraction wasn't going to end just because it made things harder.

She slid her hand over her stomach and let her mind wander. Would the baby look like Aiden?

Probably.

And her imagination was good enough for her to see the sandy-haired toddler trailing along after his father. Aiden had said he would protect their baby from his family, and he no doubt would. But while her son might have a near-perfect father, he'd be born into a very imperfect situation.

"You should be resting," Aiden said without even opening his eyes.

She wasn't sure how he even knew she was awake, but he reached for her and eased her back down next to him. Kendall lost the great view of his body, but the snuggling wasn't a bad consolation prize.

"We'll work this all out," he added. "For now, just rest."

Kendall was certain that wouldn't happen, but it didn't take long for her muscles to go slack. She could probably thank the amazing sex for that. And the fatigue that was gnawing away at her. However, she'd barely had time to close her eyes when she felt something she didn't want to feel.

The muscles in Aiden's arm tensed.

He didn't jackknife to a sitting position, but he did ease away from her, lifting his head. Obviously listening for something.

But what?

She hadn't heard anything, but Kendall certainly listened now. There were no sounds of Sarah moving around downstairs. Nothing outside, either, even though there was a breeze stirring the oaks just outside the bedroom windows.

"What's wrong?" she whispered, her heart already in her throat.

Aiden listened some more and finally shook his head. "I thought I heard the horses."

Kendall hadn't heard them at all through the night, but then the barn, corral and pasture were a good twenty yards from the house.

Aiden eased his head back onto the pillow just as Kendall heard a sound. He heard it, too, because it got him not just off the pillow but out of bed.

It was indeed one of the horses, maybe more, making a whinnying sound.

Aiden pulled on his jeans as he made his way to the window. Kendall got up as well, but he motioned for her to stay back. She did, but when Aiden stood there for several long seconds, she decided to get dressed.

Just in case.

Sadly, their *just in case* could turn out to be something bad.

"Do you see anyone?" she asked.

Another wait before he shook his head, but he kept his attention pinned to whatever was going on outside the window. "Something spooked the horses."

Because she'd spent a lot of time on a ranch, Kendall knew there were plenty of things that could do that. The area had coyotes who sometimes ventured closer to the animals, but with the awful things that had happened to Aiden and her, Kendall automatically thought the worst.

Another kidnapper could be out there, ready to come for her.

She finished putting on her clothes, and even though she stayed back, Kendall went closer to see if she could get a glimpse of anything. The moon was full and bright, casting shadows on the ground.

One of those shadows moved, causing her heart to slam against her chest.

She made a strangled sound and stepped back just as Aiden cursed and grabbed his shirt.

"It could be a kid pulling a prank," he said. But Aiden didn't sound as if he believed that any more than she did.

He threw on his clothes, grabbed his gun and headed for the door. Kendall hadn't thought her anxiety could go any higher, but that did it.

"You're not going out there," she insisted.

Aiden dropped a kiss on her mouth as if that were the cure for everything, and he opened the bedroom door. "You're waiting inside with Sarah."

So he was indeed going out there. Alone. And with the moving shadow that could be an armed thug.

Kendall hurried down the stairs behind him, but before Aiden could even knock on Sarah's door, the deputy had already opened it. "I heard your footsteps on the stairs," Sarah said. She was already dressed. Armed, too. But maybe she'd slept that way.

"Keep an eye on Kendall," he said, giving Kendall another kiss. Probably because he figured it would stop her from arguing with him.

It didn't.

"You should wait until you call for backup," Kendall suggested.

But she was talking to herself, because Aiden was already heading for the front door so he could disengage the security system.

"Reset this when I'm out," Aiden said to Sarah. He grabbed a flashlight from a table in the entry. "The security code's one-eight-six-three. And call Leland to let him know I might have a problem."

Sarah nodded, and as soon as Aiden was outside, the deputy punched in the code to reset it. She also motioned for Kendall to follow her back into the hall and took out her phone. To call Leland, no doubt.

Kendall wished they could at least go into the living

room so she might be able to catch a glimpse of Aiden outside the window, but before she could suggest that to Sarah, the deputy mumbled, "What the heck?"

"What's wrong?" Kendall asked.

"My cell phone's not working." She hurried to the kitchen and picked up the landline that was mounted on the wall. Kendall knew from the way the deputy's face dropped that it wasn't good news. "It's not working, either."

Oh, mercy.

That couldn't be good, and Kendall doubted that it was a coincidence. Someone had likely jammed the lines, and that someone was out there.

With Aiden.

"We have to tell Aiden," Kendall insisted. "He could be attacked."

Sarah nodded, then glanced around as if trying to figure out what to do. "If I open the living room window to shout out to him, the security alarm will go off. So I'll have you disarm it just long enough for me to tell him what's going on."

Now it was Kendall's turn to nod, and she hurried to the keypad on the wall next to the front door. Thankfully, unlike in her own house, there were no sidelight windows, and the door was solid wood.

"Now," Sarah said, reaching for the window.

However, reaching for it was as far as she got. Because before Kendall had even touched the keypad, she heard the beeps. Sounds coming from the security system.

"What happened?" Sarah asked. "I haven't opened the window yet."

The entry was dark, and it was hard to see, but Kendall pulled down the flap on the keypad and saw the lights. Indications of where the sensors had been armed on all the doors and windows. They were green.

Except for one.

It was red and blinking, causing the sound that was pulsing through the house.

"Someone's breaking in," Sarah said on a rise of breath.

Yes, and according to the red light, that someone was coming in through the back door.

THE HORSES WERE definitely spooked. Aiden had three mares, two fillies and a stallion in the corrals and pasture, and all were prancing and snorting. Someone had invaded their territory.

But who, and where the heck was the intruder?

Aiden had seen that shadow from his bedroom window, but he darn sure didn't see anything now. Once Leland got out here, they could divide up the area and have a look around, but not now. He didn't want to leave Kendall and Sarah alone until he was sure they weren't about to be attacked again.

He turned, intending to head back to the house, but something on the ground caught his eye.

Footprints.

He fanned the flashlight over them. They looked fresh. Too fresh, since this was a spot where the horses usually went back and forth to the water trough.

Somebody had been out here.

Aiden turned, hurrying back to the house and trying to keep watch at the same time. He still didn't see anyone, but he heard something.

The beeps from the security system.

Someone had tripped it. Maybe Sarah hadn't reset it properly after he left. Maybe.

But that seemed way too much to hope for.

He was almost back to the front porch when he heard something else. No more beeps. The security system started to blare. His gun was already drawn, and he wasn't exactly strolling, but that got him moving even faster.

The front door was still locked, and he wasn't sure if that was a good sign or not. "Open up," he called out to Sarah.

Nothing.

Not only didn't she answer, but he also didn't hear anyone coming to open the door. Definitely not good. While he kept watch around him, Aiden fished out his keys, unlocked the door and cautiously stepped inside. He spotted Sarah and Kendall almost immediately in the hall.

Thank God.

They were all right, though Sarah was standing in front of Kendall. The deputy, too, had pulled her gun, and she motioned toward the kitchen. Aiden didn't see anyone in that general direction, but he didn't have a full view of the kitchen, either. Someone could be in there. Someone responsible for tripping the security system.

While he kept watch, Aiden punched in the code to turn off the blaring alarm so he could listen for anyone inside the house. Hard to hear, though, over the sound of his own heartbeat crashing in his ears.

This couldn't be happening again. Kendall and the baby couldn't be in danger. Maybe this was literally a false alarm.

But Aiden had to ditch that hope fast.

The front door was open just a fraction. Enough for him to hear a strange sound out in the front yard. Since this could be some kind of diversion, he motioned for Sarah to keep watch of the kitchen, and he glanced behind him. The sound turned to more of a crackle, and while he watched, both his truck and Sarah's cruiser burst into flames.

Hell.

Not just little fires, either. These were full light-ups. As he didn't smell any accelerants, that meant someone had likely put some kind of incendiary devices on them. It also meant Aiden couldn't use the vehicles to get Sarah and Kendall out of there.

Time to do something other than just stand around and wait for something bad to happen, because the *bad* had already started.

"I'm Sheriff Braddock," he called out to whoever might be in the house. He eased the front door shut so that he wouldn't be ambushed from behind. "If you have a weapon, put it down and come out so I can see you."

He didn't expect that order to work. And it didn't.

Certainly no one surrendered a weapon or stepped out. But he did hear someone moving around in the direction of the back door. Aiden figured that with the break-in and the fires, the intruder wasn't leaving.

Aiden hurried across the entry, fully expecting someone to fire a shot at him. He thanked his lucky stars that it didn't happen, and he joined Sarah and Kendall in the narrow hall. Both were unharmed as far as he could tell, but Kendall had her hand over her stomach and was looking many steps past the terrified stage.

"He set the vehicles on fire?" Kendall asked in a whisper.

Aiden nodded.

"And I tried to call for backup, but the phone lines are jammed," Sarah added. "I can't get in touch with Leland."

That was *not* what Aiden wanted to hear. It wasn't hard to jam lines, but along with the fires, it meant whoever was behind this was serious about kidnapping Kendall again. If the person had simply wanted them dead, he could have set fire to the house and then shot them when they ran outside. Heck, he could have gunned down Aiden, too, when he went to check on the horses.

But he hadn't.

Why?

If the goal was just to get Kendall or kill them all, then why hadn't this idiot already struck?

"Are you waiting for your boss to arrive?" Aiden called out.

Yeah, taunting this guy probably wasn't smart, but he wanted to hear something, anything, to pinpoint his location.

And to make sure he wasn't outside setting fire to the house.

Again, there was no answer. Well, no verbal one anyway, but again Aiden heard somebody moving around in there.

"Take Kendall into the bathroom," Aiden whispered to the deputy. "I'll see what this guy is up to."

Kendall frantically shook her head. "You don't have backup."

True, and he might not get it. But at least he had Sarah to protect Kendall. Now he needed to eliminate any possible danger so he could get Kendall the heck out of there and to a safe house.

Aiden was about to insist that Sarah and she get going to the bathroom. Not ideal, but the tiles would better protect them if bullets started flying. However, the moment he opened his mouth, he heard something else. And this time it wasn't coming from the kitchen.

But rather the guest room. The same area where he'd been about to send Kendall and Sarah.

It sounded as if someone was coming through the window.

"Change of plans," Aiden whispered. "The three of us are getting out of here now."

The question was—which way? There were fires in the front of the house. Someone was in the kitchen by the back door. Someone else was about to come at them from the hall. That didn't exactly leave many options, and none of them was a sure thing when it came to keeping Kendall out of harm's way.

He looked around, his attention landing on the side window. Away from the fires, away from the back door. And that probably meant the brains behind this had already figured out that it was the escape route Aiden would take.

In other words, a trap.

Even though he hated to do this, Aiden figured their best chance of survival was eliminating the threats one by one. And to do that, it meant taking Kendall with him and Sarah into the lion's den.

"Come on," he whispered to them.

Aiden headed toward the kitchen, knowing that he was about to face down yet another hired gun.

Chapter Seventeen

With each step that they took toward the kitchen, Kendall's heart raced even harder.

Her thoughts were racing, too. This could turn deadly fast, and with the vehicles now on fire, it meant they would have to escape on foot. As it was still dark outside, there could be even more hired guns waiting to attack.

First, though, they had to deal with the two thugs who might already be inside the house. That pair would be more than enough to finish what had already been set in motion.

Aiden was ahead of her. Sarah behind. Both were armed, but Kendall wished she had a gun. It was too late for her to try to grab one, so maybe they could get out of this without shots being fired.

Of course, they hadn't managed to avoid violence with the other attacks, and because of it, four men were now dead. Too bad that body count hadn't stopped their boss from hiring yet another crew to do the job where the others had failed.

Kendall kept her hands over her stomach. Not that her hands would do much if someone did start shooting at them. But she had to do something to protect the baby, and this was all she had.

Aiden inched them across the living room, past the very spot where days earlier the other two gunmen had held her captive, waiting for Aiden to come home. Kendall had no idea how long she'd been forced to kneel on that floor. It'd felt like hours before Aiden finally arrived.

Despite the gunshot wound, he'd managed to rescue her, and while she hated relying on anyone to do that for her again, if she needed a rescuer, she preferred it to be Aiden. Other than her, no one else would fight harder to keep their baby safe.

Their baby.

Not a good time for the image of that ultrasound to skip through her mind. It only revved up her heartbeat and breathing even more. She didn't need that. She needed to focus in case there was some way she could help Sarah and Aiden.

They walked past the sofa, and Aiden focused his attention ahead while Sarah kept watch behind them. There was no one in the living room. No sounds to indicate the intruders were still in the house, but she doubted they'd just leave without getting what they had come there to get.

And what they no doubt intended to get was her.

But why?

Why did this keep happening?

Too bad she might finally know the answer when it was too late to do anything about it, but she figured it had something to do with the evidence against Jewell. Or maybe the person behind this wanted to silence her for good.

Aiden stopped just short of the entry into the kitchen and glanced around. There were half walls that divided the living room from the kitchen, but toward the back door was also a pantry and laundry room. Someone could be lurking there.

"Hell," Aiden cursed.

Kendall's heart went to her knees. So did she, because Aiden pushed her down and took cover behind the wall. He also aimed his gun at something or somebody toward the back door.

"Come out with your hands up," Aiden snarled.

Kendall didn't hear any indication the person was doing that.

Sarah stayed on her feet, hovering over Kendall while she continued to keep watch all around them. Kendall looked, too, and listened.

Did she hear someone breathing?

If the intruder was there, then why hadn't he just fired at them?

"Behind you, Sarah!" Aiden shouted.

Even though Sarah had been keeping watch in that direction, she obviously hadn't seen the intruder in the shadows. She snapped toward the living room, already aiming her gun.

"Wouldn't pull that trigger if I were you," the man said.

Like all the other attackers, he was wearing a ski mask, and he had a gun pointed right at them.

Or rather right at Kendall.

"We can do this the easy way," the man continued, "and Miss O'Neal can come with us."

"That's not gonna happen," Aiden snapped. "But you can make this easy on yourself by surrendering."

Kendall couldn't be certain, but she thought the guy might have chuckled. Probably because surrendering was the last thing on his mind, but he had to have known that Aiden wasn't just going to let her walk out of there with a kidnapper.

"You don't have a way out of this," someone else said.

Yet another man, and this was the one in the kitchen.

Kendall couldn't see him, but she figured he was on the other side of the fridge. Behind cover. So even if Aiden shot the one in the living room, this one would be there to continue the attack.

"You're not taking Kendall," Aiden growled.

"Oh, no?" That came from the guy in the living room. "You'll want to rethink that."

Before Kendall could even consider what to do or say, Aiden shoved her to the side of a chair and turned, pointing his gun at the guy in the kitchen. Sarah took aim at the one in the living room.

"Don't shoot!" someone called out.

Not the voice of the thugs. This was a woman, and Kendall immediately recognized who it was.

Carla.

Aiden and Sarah both froze, and because Kendall didn't want to distract Aiden by leaving cover, she just pulled in her breath and held it. Waiting and praying.

God, no.

Of course, she'd known all along that Carla could be the one behind this, but it was another thing to have it confirmed. Aiden had to be falling apart inside, but he kept his gun and aim steady.

"What are you doing here?" he asked his mother.

Carla made a rough sobbing sound. "Please, just put down your gun. If not, they'll kill you."

Now Aiden reacted. His nostrils flared, and his teeth came together. "You'd really have them kill your own son?" he snapped.

Silence. For what seemed an eternity.

Sarah volleyed glances between the living room, Aiden and the kitchen. She was clearly waiting for Aiden to tell her what to do, but Aiden stayed silent as well, glaring at his mother.

But then he flinched.

Aiden's grimace changed, and a single word of profanity slipped from his mouth. Even Sarah turned to the kitchen to gape and stare.

"I'm sorry," Carla said, her voice barely audible. "But if you shoot, they'll kill me, then you."

Kendall didn't get up, but she did lift her head slightly so she could take a quick look over the half wall. She wanted to see what had grabbed Aiden's and Sarah's attention.

And she soon saw what.

Carla was there all right, partly hidden in the shadows of the dark kitchen. Her face was stark white, and she appeared to be trembling. She wasn't armed.

But the person standing behind her was.

That person had a gun aimed right at Carla's head.

AIDEN HADN'T THOUGHT this night could get any worse, but obviously he'd been dead wrong about that.

"Hell." And because Aiden didn't know what else to say, he repeated it.

When Aiden had first seen his mother in the kitchen, he thought for certain that she was in on this latest kidnapping plan. After all, she had motive, means and opportunity. Well, motive if he counted her wanting to get back at Jewell and her family by making them look guilty as sin of trying to destroy evidence. However, with the missing money and news of her being in a mental hospital, Carla had gone to the top of his suspect list.

She didn't look so much like a suspect now.

Unless she was faking all this so she could clear her name. Anything was possible, including that.

"Are you in on this?" Aiden asked her.

No sound of outrage or drama from his mother. She just shook her head as tears trickled down her cheeks. It was hard to push those tears aside, but Aiden still wasn't convinced she was innocent.

"I'm going to fire a shot at that jerk behind you," Aiden said to Carla. "And since he's already said he'll fire back, now would be a good time for you to come clean of any of your own wrongdoing."

Carla shook her head. "Please don't shoot. He'll kill you."

"Yeah, I will," the guy verified. "I'll kill her, too. Saving her isn't part of the plan. In fact, the only one I'm supposed to save for sure is the pregnant woman."

If Aiden could have believed this guy, it would have made him feel a little better to know that Kendall could be spared. But the idiot was a hired gun, and even if killing her wasn't in the plan, that didn't mean it wouldn't happen.

Kendall touched her fingers to her mouth, both her hands and lips trembling. Yes, she was afraid. So was Aiden. But he also saw the fire in her eyes. She wasn't giving up without a fight.

That was both bad and good.

Good because he might need her help in the next couple of minutes. Help that might include her running for cover somewhere else in the house. But he didn't want the fire in her eyes spurring her to get in the middle of this fight.

"I want you to think of the baby first," he whispered to Kendall.

Oh, that didn't sit well with her, but he could see that it sank in. Good. She'd run if it came down to it, and Aiden was afraid that it would. Now he only hoped Sarah could eliminate the thug in the living room. While he was hoping, Aiden didn't want there to be any other hired guns waiting outside.

These two along with his mother were plenty enough.

"This is a little bit of déjà vu for me." Aiden motioned around the living room. "The last time two clowns tried to kidnap Kendall, that didn't work out so well for them. So, is that your plan, to die tonight like they did?"

"I've got your mother," the one in the kitchen growled. "You'll cooperate."

Carla's mouth tightened. "Clearly, you don't know the strained relationship between me and my son. He's not going to put protecting me over his unborn child. And he shouldn't."

If she meant that, it was a sentiment that Aiden had never expected to hear coming from her, and later, he'd thank her for it. For now, though, that was still a big *if.*

"I'm a good shot," Aiden said to the man. "And since you're a head taller than my mother, it won't be hard taking you out. Even if you try to scrunch down." He hiked his thumb to Sarah. "My deputy's a good shot, too. You want to test that, or do you two just want to put down your guns right now?"

The guy in the kitchen laughed. "He said you had a smart mouth, and he was right."

Aiden picked right up on that. *"He?"*

"He," the guy verified without clarifying it. "Now, here's the way this is really going to work. If the O'Neal woman doesn't come with us, then we start shooting. First, your mother. Then you and the deputy."

So the three of them were expendable, making him wonder who they'd nab to destroy evidence. If that was still what they wanted to do, that is. Maybe there were new rules now.

"Your plan sucks," Aiden insisted. "How soon do you

think I'll leave you alive once you've pulled the trigger? You'll have a bullet in your head before my mother hits the floor."

Aiden knew it sounded cold and uncaring. He had to be right now. Because if he showed any fear or any indication that he would back down, then it'd start a gunfight. Not only would his mother be killed, maybe Sarah, too, but a stray bullet could hit Kendall.

"Who's behind this?" Aiden asked his mother. "And if it's you, I want to know now."

"It's not me." Carla's voice cracked on the last word.

Aiden hoped he didn't regret it later, but he believed her, and that meant if she hadn't hired these men, somebody else had. Somebody with plenty of money and enough hatred for him and his family that he didn't mind seeing them die.

"I can't say anything else," his mother added in a mumble.

The gunman behind her touched his finger to the communicator that was in his ear and then cursed. "Time to put an end to this now!"

He no longer sounded cocky, just nervous that this wasn't going down as planned. Well, Aiden wasn't too easy about it, either, but he was damned if he did and damned if he didn't. He couldn't shoot without risking Kendall's, Sarah's and his mother's lives, and he couldn't let these goons take Kendall.

"No," Aiden said, and he didn't mumble it, either. "If you want to try to take Kendall, you have to come through me."

That didn't please the masked guy because his profanity went up a notch, and it took Aiden a moment before he realized the hired gun wasn't the only one talking.

He heard another voice. This one coming from his back porch.

"Hell, kill them all," the man said. "Burn the place to the ground so I can finish this."

And Aiden recognized the voice of the man who'd just ordered their murders.

Chapter Eighteen

Lee Palmer.

Kendall knew she shouldn't have been surprised to hear Palmer's voice. After all, he was a suspect. But it was the first time she'd heard him speak with such venom toward her.

Kill them all.

Kendall lifted her head, staring at him, and she knew this wasn't a bluff. Palmer wanted them all dead, including her precious baby.

That realization got Kendall standing so she could face him down. By God, if he was going to try to kill them, she wanted to know why. She also wanted to know if Carla was in on this. One look at Aiden's mom, though, and Kendall was thinking no. The woman seemed just as terrified as Kendall.

"Why are you doing this?" Kendall demanded, staring at Palmer.

Some of that venom faded from Palmer's expression, and he even made a weary sigh. "Killing you wasn't part of the plan, Kendall. Sorry that you got caught up in this mess."

The apology didn't help matters at all, and the anger rippled through her. Apparently through Aiden, too, because he looked ready to tear Palmer limb from limb. Kendall wouldn't have minded that happening, but she didn't want Aiden hurt in the process. And he would be hurt, since Palmer and his thugs had their guns aimed at him.

Three guns against Aiden's and Sarah's two were not good odds. Heck, there were no good odds when it came to her baby and these killers.

"Why?" Kendall repeated to Palmer.

Aiden inched closer to her, no doubt so he could be in a better position to protect her when the attack finally happened.

"This all got out of hand," Palmer finally said. "Yost and his partner weren't supposed to shoot you. They were only supposed to make Aiden destroy those bone fragments so your sister could get out of that jail cell."

Kendall desperately wanted Jewell free but not like this. "Jewell wouldn't want that evidence destroyed."

Palmer lifted his shoulder. "Well, I was helping her out, wasn't I? She always was a little too goody-goody for me, but hey, any woman who sliced up Whitt Braddock and left his body to rot is a friend of mine. I figured I owed her a favor or two."

This had to be hard for Aiden to take, but he didn't respond to Palmer. He only moved closer to her. Maybe that meant Aiden had a plan to try to get them out of this.

"Like I said," Palmer went on, "I'm sorry you got caught up in this. If Yost hadn't told you that I'd hired him, we wouldn't be here right now."

Kendall froze. Shook her head. "He didn't tell me."

Palmer studied her as if trying to decide if she was telling the truth, then he cursed. "Well, he said he did, and I believed him. I couldn't take that chance, could I? Especially since Yost was stupid enough to drive out to my place and get it all captured on that traffic camera. Coming to my place wasn't part of the plan."

"But he panicked," Aiden filled in, "when I killed his partner."

"Like I said, he was stupid," Palmer added. "Couldn't risk him being out there. It was the same for that moron of a prison guard. He botched that big-time."

And now both Yost and the guard were dead. She hoped that caused the two hired guns in the house to have second thoughts about doing this, because if Palmer would kill the guard and Yost, then anyone connected to this plan would likely be eliminated.

"You set up Joplin and my mother?" Aiden asked, though she wasn't sure how he could speak with his jaw that stiff.

Palmer scowled. "*Set up* is such an ugly phrase. All I did was fix it so Joplin would show up at that meeting with Yost. It took some of the spotlight off me and put it on him."

"You set him up," Aiden confirmed. "So, Joplin didn't fire those shots at Yost. One of your hired guns no doubt did that. And I'm also betting you did that disappearing act with the money from Carla's bogus account."

No denial there, either. Heaven knew how long Palmer had been planning this, but Kendall still wasn't convinced of his reasons for doing it.

"Helping my sister seems a little extreme," Kendall said to Palmer. "Especially since we didn't ask for your help."

"He didn't do this for Jewell. He did it because Palmer hates me," Carla volunteered. "Yes, I had an affair with him. If you can call what a teenager does an affair. I was stupid, and I paid dearly for that stupidity." She paused. "In addition to the settlement money he got for my car rage *incident*, he extorted money from my family. That's how Palmer got so rich."

Kendall glanced at Aiden to see if he knew that. He apparently didn't. "Palmer was the one who was engaged at the time, not you," Aiden reminded her. "So, how could he have extorted more money?"

Palmer smiled. "Tell him, Carla. I'm sure your son will want to hear all about this."

And Kendall was equally certain that he wouldn't. Still, it sounded as if this was all at the heart of what was going on now.

Carla took a deep breath. "Palmer made sex tapes of us. I didn't know," she added. "But when he broke things off with me, he told my father he'd mail copies of the tapes to all our friends and family if we didn't pay up. So we paid him a hundred thousand dollars."

Definitely not petty cash, especially forty years ago.

"Palmer gave us the tapes," Carla continued. "We destroyed them, and I thought that was the last of it. Then, when I married Whitt, Palmer came around demanding more money. He had copies of the tapes."

Palmer didn't deny any of that, but the smile did vanish from his face. "What Carla left out was that Whitt hired some muscle to break into my house. They beat me within an inch of my life until I told them where I'd hidden the tapes, and then they stole them."

It took Kendall a moment to process all that. Aiden was obviously a few seconds ahead of her, because he cursed.

"This is why you have a vendetta against my family?" Aiden snapped.

Again, Palmer didn't deny it, but it was clear that was the reason. "Hey, I'm not the only one with a vendetta. Remember, your daddy was always trying to butt heads with me over any little thing. I kept besting him, and it riled him. That, and his getting my *leftovers*."

With that, Palmer aimed a smug glance at Carla. A glance that nobody, including Carla, missed.

A sound of raw anger came from Aiden's throat, and Kendall was afraid he would just launch himself at Palmer. Kendall had never cared much for Palmer, but she could see now the true monster that he was.

Carla had almost certainly already seen the monster a time or two, and the sound that Aiden made was nothing compared to her shriek of outrage.

"Yeah, leftovers," Palmer repeated.

Kendall could have bet it was a bad idea to throw that in Carla's face. And it was. Maybe a bad idea for all of them.

Because Carla turned and launched herself at Palmer.

"STOP!" AIDEN YELLED to his mother.

But he was already too late to try to diffuse this. Carla rammed right into Palmer, and despite the fact that the man outweighed her by a good fifty pounds, it was enough to off-balance him.

Both his mother and Palmer fell to the floor, where they started a wrestling match.

That was only the beginning of the chaos.

The hired gun in the kitchen ducked out of the way so he wouldn't get knocked down on the floor, too, but as soon as he recovered, he whipped around and aimed his weapon at Aiden.

"Get down," Aiden told Kendall, not waiting for her to do that. He pushed her to the floor and tried to move in front of her as best he could.

Right before the blast echoed through the room.

The idiot in the living room had fired at him, and if

Aiden had been just a split second slower, he wouldn't have gotten Kendall out of the way in time. That riled him to the core, but he was more than just riled.

He was scared that he wouldn't be able to get them out of this alive.

Sarah fired at the shooter in the living room, all of them scrambling to take cover. Kendall and he landed next to the chair. Sarah behind the sofa. Aiden lost sight of the guy in the kitchen, but the one who'd fired darted out into the entry.

Just out of range for Aiden to blast him to smithereens. How dare this moron try to kill Kendall and the baby?

Another bullet came barreling past him.

Not from the guy in the entry this time. It'd come from the kitchen, and the bullet landed just a fraction away from Sarah. Thankfully, his deputy hurried to the other end of the sofa, and she came up ready to fire.

So did Aiden.

There was no way his mother could hold off Palmer for long, and like his hired guns, Palmer was armed. Considering that he'd called Carla his "leftovers," Aiden doubted that the man would spare her life.

Or anyone else's for that matter.

No, Palmer probably had plans to kill all of them, including these two that he'd hired.

"Stay down," Aiden whispered to Kendall.

Even though the seconds were ticking away, Aiden took a moment to glance at her and make sure she was okay. She wasn't. Kendall wasn't hurt, thank God, but she was shaking and clearly terrified.

"Do you have a backup weapon I can use?" she asked.

Okay, maybe not as terrified as he thought. Aiden didn't like the idea of putting a gun in her hands, because it might make the hired pair zoom in on her as a target. But like him and the others, Kendall was already a target, and it was best if she had a way to protect herself.

"I still want you to stay down," he insisted, but he removed the small gun from his boot holster and handed it to her. Aiden added a firm glance, hoping that Kendall would listen.

The gunman in the kitchen fired another shot at Sarah, and since he was focusing on the deputy, that meant he probably figured his boss could take care of a middle-aged woman like Carla. But his mother was holding her own. She rammed her knee into Palmer's groin and had the man howling in pain.

That distraction wouldn't last, either.

After all, Palmer still had hold of his gun, and he was trying to aim it at Carla so he could shoot her.

Aiden had to do something, fast, and that something started with getting rid of the shooter in the kitchen. The guy had Sarah pinned down. Plus, the one in the entry could get in on this at any second.

"Watch behind me," he said to Kendall because he had no other choice. He needed to get in a better position, and he couldn't risk doing that if the guy was going to shoot him in the back. If that happened, Kendall's chance of survival would go down significantly.

Kendall shifted her position, still staying down, but she aimed in the direction of the entry. Aiden aimed at the kitchen. He leaned out but immediately had to duck back when the shooter sent another bullet his way.

From the corner of Aiden's eye, he saw Sarah maneuvering herself for a better shot as well, but Aiden waved her off and instead motioned toward the entry. He wanted Kendall and Sarah to focus on that, since there were two guns in the kitchen.

His mother screamed, a bloodcurdling sound that

knifed right through Aiden. No, Carla hadn't exactly been mother of the year, but it sounded as if Palmer was killing her.

Aiden moved out of cover again, taking aim at the hired gun.

The hired gun did the same to him.

But Aiden pulled the trigger first.

The bullet smacked into the guy's chest, and because the shooter was still lifting his gun toward the living room, Aiden was forced to fire a second shot at him. That one sent the guy to the floor.

"Stay back," Aiden warned Kendall one last time.

He raced into the kitchen, and the first thing he saw was the blood on his mother's face. Palmer had obviously hit her, but she was still fighting, and she had a tight grip on his right wrist.

But not tight enough.

Before Aiden could even get to her, Palmer turned the gun and pulled the trigger. The shot didn't go into his mother, but it came right at Aiden. He had to dive to the floor.

And it wasn't the only shot.

Behind him, Sarah shouted, "Watch out!"

Aiden scrambled to the side of the kitchen, only to realize that Sarah wasn't yelling at him.

But rather at Kendall.

Aiden's heart slammed so hard in his chest that it felt as if his ribs had cracked. The shooter had his gun aimed right at Kendall, and even though she was hunched down, he had a direct shot to kill her.

"No!" Aiden called out, hoping to get the guy's attention off Kendall.

It didn't work.

The shot tore through the room.

Chapter Nineteen

The shot was so deafening that it drowned out everything else. Aiden was shouting something to her, but exactly what Kendall didn't know.

From the corner of her eye, she could see Aiden hurrying toward her. Sarah, too. But they stopped, their attention rifling to the gunman in the entry. At least, he'd been in the entry just seconds earlier.

Now he was tumbling to the living room floor.

Because Kendall had shot him.

Oh, God. Not another one. That was the only thing that registered in her mind when she saw that the man was still moving. And not just moving. Even though there was blood on the front of his shirt, he was trying to aim his gun at her again.

Aiden fixed that.

He tore across the room, kicking the gun out of the man's hand, and pointed his gun at him. "Move and you die," Aiden said, and there was nothing in his voice to indicate he was bluffing.

The guy stopped, groaned and rolled onto his back, clutching his chest. Kendall could see that he was bleeding, but it didn't look as life-threatening as she'd originally thought. The bullet appeared to have caught him in the shoulder.

"Watch him," Aiden told Sarah, and he hurried to Kendall. "Are you all right?"

She planned on lying, telling him that she was fine. She wasn't, not by a long shot. But the sound coming from the kitchen stopped her from saying anything.

"No!" Carla said. Not a shout, but Kendall could hear the heavy emotion in the woman's voice.

Kendall turned, dreading what she might see. It seemed a horrible thought to wish a person dead, but she was hoping she would see Palmer lying next to the gunman whom Aiden had killed.

But he wasn't.

Palmer was on his feet, but he'd still somehow managed to keep hold of his gun. A gun that he now had pointed at Carla's head.

"Let go of her," Aiden insisted.

Palmer chuckled. "I'm thinking the answer to that is no."

He sounded cocky again despite the fact he looked as if he'd lost that fight with Carla. The woman had clawed at his face and left streaks of blood on his cheeks. He must have been in pain, but he certainly didn't show it.

Unlike Carla.

Aiden's mother had her teeth clamped over her bottom lip, and she was wincing. Probably because Palmer had managed to hit her multiple times. There were bruises already forming on her face.

"It's over," Aiden said. He kept his left hand braced on his shooting wrist and inched closer to Carla and Palmer. "There's no way you can get out of this."

Palmer's smile said differently. "Are you forgetting I have a hostage?"

"Are you forgetting that every cop in the state will be looking for you?" Aiden countered.

"Maybe not," Palmer mumbled.

And that answer chilled Kendall to the bone.

Because it didn't sound as if he was worried at all about being caught. Probably because he'd already arranged to kill them all.

Aiden must have realized that, too, because he glanced back at the injured man. "Sarah, ask him if there are any firebombs set in the house or if there are other gunmen waiting outside. If he doesn't answer, beat him until he tells you."

Yes, it was harsh, but they had to know. Kendall wanted nothing more than to get out of there with Aiden, Sarah and Carla, but that wasn't going to happen unless they got that gun away from Palmer and they made sure it was safe. After all, Palmer had already hired plenty of men to come after them, so he could have planted others to make sure he carried out his plan.

"I'm leaving with your mother," Palmer insisted.

Sarah grabbed the injured gunman, dragged him onto the sofa and snapped him right to her face. "What's out there? What did your boss do?"

"And remember, Palmer's not saying a thing about taking you with him," Aiden added when the guy attempted a smile.

"Come on." Palmer grabbed hold of Carla and started backing out the door with her in tow. He no longer wore that cocky smile, which meant he was perhaps worried about what his hired gun was going to tell them.

"You're leaving me here?" the guy shouted.

But Palmer ignored him and kept moving.

The gunman spat out some profanity and came off the sofa to face his boss. "There's one more guy waiting on a ranch trail about a quarter of a mile from here. He's in an SUV, and it's the getaway car."

"What about explosives?" Aiden pressed.

"None. And I would have been the one to set them." He added some more profanity, aimed at Palmer.

If Palmer even heard him, he didn't react. Not at first anyway. Then, without warning, he took aim at the man and shot him. Just as quickly, Palmer put the gun back against Carla's head.

"Can't have anybody talking," Palmer threatened. "Now, can I?"

Yes, he was definitely planning on killing them all. But how? Had the dead man been wrong about more fire-bombs?

Palmer moved his grip from Carla's arm to her hair and pulled her out onto the porch with him. Kendall didn't know where this ranch trail was exactly, but if Palmer somehow managed to clear the barn, there were plenty of trees back there that he could use to hide and escape.

"This one's dead," Sarah said, touching her fingers to the gunman's neck.

Again, no reaction from Palmer. Not that Kendall expected one. He'd just shot a man in cold blood.

Aiden used the appliances and cabinets for cover, following Palmer inch for inch until he reached the back porch. When Kendall tried to follow, Aiden motioned for Sarah to get in front of her, and the deputy did.

Protecting Kendall, again.

She hated that she had to put someone else's life in danger, but she also had to think of her baby.

There were flagstone steps leading to the unfenced backyard, and that was exactly where Palmer headed. Sarah stopped in the doorway, and Aiden made his way out to the porch. Kendall had her attention focused just on them, and that was why she nearly missed the slight snapping sound behind her.

She whirled around.

And the man was there. Another gunman wearing a ski mask. He put his gun not to her head but to her stomach.

"I thought you might need help," the man called out to Palmer.

Aiden pivoted around, the color blanching from his face. No doubt because he saw the new threat. The gun pointed at her.

"Get out on the porch with the sheriff," the newcomer told Sarah.

Sarah volleyed some glances between Aiden and the gunman, and Aiden finally nodded. She didn't hurry to join him, but when she made her way there, she turned her gun toward the new attacker.

While Palmer continued to drag Carla across the yard.

It was still dark and it was hard to think or see with her pulse racing a mile a minute, but Kendall knew they didn't have much time. Once Palmer cleared the yard, this monster would kill Aiden, Sarah and her. Palmer would take care of Carla. If Palmer did manage to destroy all the evidence, then he could get off scot-free.

"I'm not going to let you kill my son and that baby," Carla spat out.

Without warning, she dropped to the ground. Palmer fired, but Kendall didn't see where the bullet went. That's because the goon behind Kendall grabbed her. No doubt ready to shoot her. And he would have done just that.

If Aiden hadn't come right at him.

There was a rage in Aiden's eyes. All aimed at the scum holding her.

Kendall managed to get out of the way, barely, and Aiden rammed his full weight into the guy. There was another shot. Not from this goon, Kendall realized. It'd come from the yard.

"Help my mother," Aiden said to Sarah, and he stripped the gun from the man's hand and body-slammed the gunman against the wall.

Hard.

So hard that it rattled the porch.

The guy made a guttural gasping sound. Clearly Aiden had knocked the breath out of him, and he also slammed his fist into the man's face. Not once but three times. Before Aiden latched on to him and dragged him into the yard.

Carla was sprawled on the ground, and Sarah was struggling with Palmer, trying to disarm the man. However, Aiden pulled her off him and grabbed Palmer as he'd done with the gunman.

Kendall's breath was already thin, and that robbed her of what little she had. For a moment, she thought Aiden might kill Palmer right then, right there.

But he didn't.

"You're under arrest," Aiden said, reaching for Palmer's gun.

An oily smile bent Palmer's mouth, and there was a loud blast.

Oh, God.

A gunshot.

"Aiden!" Kendall shouted, hurrying down the porch.

A thousand things went through her head. None good. Palmer had managed to shoot Aiden, and now he'd die without knowing how she felt about him. Without ever having seen his son.

"I'm okay," Aiden managed to say when she flung herself into his arms.

And he was.

However, she couldn't say the same for Palmer. With that sick smile still on his face, he crumpled to the ground, the gun falling out of his hand.

The gun Palmer had used to kill himself.

"Sarah, call an ambulance," Aiden said, and she felt the muscles in his arm go stiff. He also moved away from her.

That's when Kendall saw the blood.

Carla had been shot.

Chapter Twenty

Aiden felt as if he'd been through a war. A war that wasn't over yet.

Yes, Palmer was dead, most of his hired guns, too, and Kendall and the baby were no longer in danger. But that danger had ended with a high price tag.

His mother was unconscious in a hospital bed after having had surgery, and Kendall looked as if she might faint at any moment. That's why Aiden had tried multiple times to make her sit down, but she'd insisted on waiting in the hall outside his mother's room.

Maybe because Kendall felt that Carla wouldn't want her in there.

Or maybe because Kendall wanted some distance from his mother and him.

Aiden couldn't blame her. He'd always thought of himself as a damn good lawman, but here he hadn't been able to stop four attacks on Kendall. Any one of which could have left her dead.

Just the thought of it twisted his stomach into a hard knot.

It probably wasn't doing much for Kendall's stomach, either. Or the baby. Thank God his son wouldn't remember any of this, but it would stay with Kendall, his mother and him for a lifetime.

"Your sister Shelby is on the way," Leland said, sticking his head in the door of the hospital room. "She was in Houston, and she'll get here as fast as she can."

Good. His other sister, Laine, was already there in the waiting room, and once Carla woke up, it would probably help to see her kids.

Probably.

There was a good chance that Carla would want to wash her hands of him. A good chance that he'd want to wash his hands of her, too, if she didn't have a change of heart about Kendall and the baby.

With that thought, Aiden moved away from his mother's hospital bed and stepped out into the hall. Kendall's back was against the wall there, and she was chewing on her bottom lip.

"Is she awake?" Kendall asked.

Aiden shook his head, and because she looked as if she could use another hug, he pulled her into his arms. Something he'd been doing most of the night, and like the other times, Kendall stayed there a couple of seconds and then maneuvered away.

"I'm okay." Another repeat of what she'd already told him. "You should be with your mother."

He stared at her, wishing he had a translation for that. Even though he had two sisters, Aiden knew he didn't always interpret the signals right. And Kendall definitely seemed to be sending out some kind of signal here.

"I should be with my mother," he admitted. "But I'd like to be with you, too."

Oh, man. That sounded pretty lame, and it was a massive understatement. "I *need* to be with you," he tried again.

And that need encompassed a lot. He not only wanted her in the room with him, but he also wanted her in his arms.

"When I hold you," he said, "it makes the worst of the images disappear."

She blinked.

Aiden groaned. He was making a mess of this. "I want you in my arms for other reasons, but that's one of them."

Kendall nodded, slipped back into his embrace.

It definitely helped. Well, it helped him anyway, but he wasn't so sure Kendall was getting anything out of this.

"What can I do to make things better for you?" he asked.

She didn't move away this time, but Kendall did look up at him. "You can kiss me. When you kiss me, the worst of the images disappear."

All right. Aiden preferred a kiss to a hug anyway, so that's what he did. He kissed Kendall, probably not for all the right reasons, either. Of course, he wanted to get those nightmarish images out of her head, but kissing her was also the purest form of pleasure for him.

Like always, the heat slid right through him. Head to toe. And it helped a whole heck of a lot to push his nightmares aside, too. Nightmares of the attack anyway. But there were plenty of other things about their situation that would give him some sleepless nights.

"I could have lost both you and the baby," he said.

"But you didn't."

She kissed him again, a nice reminder that both she and the baby were okay. Aiden hadn't taken her word for that, though. Kendall had had a checkup and another ultrasound while his mother was in surgery. Thank God this latest attack and stress hadn't caused any physical harm.

His mother was a different story.

She'd come out of the surgery to remove a bullet from her chest. A bullet that Palmer had put there. If the man weren't dead, Aiden would have gone after him and made him pay. He and his mother didn't have a perfect relationship, nowhere near it, but she didn't deserve this.

Aiden heard the footsteps, and because the adrenaline was still fueling his body, he turned, ready to draw his gun. But it was just Leland, making his way down the hall toward them. Aiden hoped the deputy wasn't there to deliver bad news, because Aiden had met his quota for a lifetime or two.

Kendall started to step away, probably so that she wouldn't be in his arms while he talked to Leland, but Aiden held on. He wasn't ready to let go of her yet. Maybe not ever.

He mentally repeated that.

And then took out the *maybe*.

He had no intention of letting Kendall go, but the problem was—how did he make that happen?

"You two okay?" Leland asked, eyeing them. Maybe because of the snug embrace but also because they'd been put through the wringer and back.

Aiden nodded. "Did you get Palmer's hired gun to the jail?"

"Yeah. And he's talking. Neither of our other suspects was involved in this." Leland's gaze drifted to Carla. "And we're gathering the money trail to prove that it was all Palmer's doing."

Kendall gave a heavy sigh. "Palmer did all this because of bad blood. For revenge. And what did he get out of it? Nothing. He's dead, and we're all left to deal with the aftermath of this mess he created."

Yes, that was the problem with bad blood. It stayed bad and festered unless someone did something about it.

And that's what Aiden intended to do.

"I want us to put this bad blood aside," he said to Kendall. "If our families don't do the same, then that's on them, but I don't want this between us any longer."

She looked up at him. Smiled. Okay, it wasn't a big smile, but man, it lit up her whole face.

"And I want you to marry me," he added.

Aiden wasn't sure who was more surprised that he'd just blurted that out: Kendall, Leland or himself.

"Uh, I think I got something else to do," Leland said, making a vague motion toward the exit. "I'll call you if there are any updates."

Aiden mumbled something about that being fine, but he kept his attention on Kendall. She wasn't exactly jumping for joy over his proposal.

Of course, it'd been a lousy proposal.

"I know," he explained. "That was bad. I should have gotten down on one knee. Should have had a ring. Probably should have waited until we were in a place that didn't smell like antiseptic."

Kendall stared at him, obviously waiting for something, so he kissed her again. At first, she stayed a little stiff, but by degrees, she softened until she melted right into his arms.

Just a few days ago, Aiden had never thought of himself as the marrying kind. Not the fathering kind, either. But he was looking forward to both. At least he was if he could convince Kendall to say yes. The kiss had helped plenty, but Aiden wasn't sure he wanted her saying yes simply because they were good at kissing and falling into bed.

Though those things did help.

This time, he was the one to break the kiss so he could put his mouth to use, hopefully convincing her that marriage was the right thing to do. But he didn't get a chance to say anything, because he heard a soft moaning sound. His gaze flew to the hospital bed, and he saw that his mother was opening her eyes.

"Aiden," Carla said, her voice as weak as her hand that reached out for him.

Kendall didn't just let go of him, she nudged him in Carla's direction, and Aiden went to his mother's bedside so he could give her hand a gentle squeeze. "How are you, Mom?"

Her eyes fluttered open, and she managed a smile. She also looked past him, her attention landing on Kendall. Kendall started to back out of the doorway, but Carla motioned for her to come closer.

"I'm so sorry," Carla said.

Aiden could count on one hand how many times he'd heard his mother apologize over the years. Maybe it was the painkillers or the ordeal, but the apology was aimed at Kendall.

"This wasn't your fault," Kendall assured her. "Palmer was a sick man, and he put a very sick plan into motion." That was generous of Kendall, considering that his mother hadn't exactly been kind to her.

"A plan that Palmer wouldn't have come up with if he hadn't hated me so much." Carla groaned softly and closed her eyes.

"I'll get the doctor," Aiden insisted, but Carla caught on to his hand to stop him.

"You can do that later. For now, let's just talk for a couple of minutes." Again, her attention went to Kendall. "I don't want you to push Aiden out of your life because of the things I said." She gave Kendall's stomach a soft pat.

"If you can find it in your heart to forgive me, then I want to be a part of this baby's life."

Kendall swallowed hard, and for a moment Aiden thought she might tell Carla to take a hike. She certainly had a right to do that. But Kendall nodded.

"You're his grandmother, and I don't want this baby to experience any more fallout from bad blood."

It was a bighearted concession, and Aiden was darn thankful for it.

"You mean that?" Carla asked.

Another nod from Kendall. "No matter what happens with my sister's trial, you'll be part of this baby's life. Aiden's sisters, too. If they want to be part of his life, that is."

Tears sprang to his mother's eyes. To Kendall's, too, and while this was a moment that went a long way toward mending some fences, there was something missing.

Something huge.

Because while Kendall had agreed to include his family, she hadn't exactly extended that invitation to him. And she hadn't said a word about his marriage proposal.

"Go ahead," his mother said as if sensing he had something on his mind. "I need to rest." As if to prove her point, she closed her eyes again.

Aiden didn't intend to go far from the room, but he did want to have that talk with Kendall. He led her back into the hall, got the attention of one of the nurses and let her know that his mother had regained consciousness. While the nurse went into the room to check on Carla, Aiden took Kendall several yards away.

"Thank you for that," he started. Except the start was as far as he got. He paused, waiting to see what the verdict was on his proposal.

No verdict. Kendall stared at him. Then she huffed.

"So, you should have proposed somewhere else and gotten down on one knee. Is there anything else you should have changed?"

And with that, she kissed him again. Hard. Unlike the others, this one had a bite of anger in it.

That's when Aiden got it.

Even a semi-angry kiss with Kendall was still enjoyable, but Aiden broke away because he knew where this conversation had to go.

To the L-word.

In case he was wrong about that, Kendall quickly clarified it. "I won't marry you just because I'm pregnant with your baby."

Yep, that was confirmation, so Aiden did a turnabout and kissed her. A real kiss. No anger involved. But he made it long and hot. It went on for so long that one of the nurses cleared her throat.

Aiden ignored her. He ignored everything but Kendall.

"Would you marry me if you were in love with me?" he asked. "Let me rephrase that. Are you in love with me, Kendall?"

Her left eye narrowed a little as if she was suspicious. "Yes. I am. And I'm surprised you even had to ask."

That was mighty good to hear. "What can I say? I'm a little thick when it comes to such things."

But she loved him.

Kendall loved him!

And that made him grin like an idiot.

"I don't know why you're smiling," she said. "Yes, I'm in love with you, but that doesn't mean I'll marry you." Kendall looked him straight in the eye. "The only way I'll marry you is if you're in love with me, too."

Problem solved. "Well, heck. I guess that kiss wasn't good enough after all."

"It was plenty good enough, but you have to say it."

Judging from the look she was giving him, Kendall probably thought he would choke on the words. But this was the easiest thing he'd ever done.

"I'm in love with you, Kendall. Have been since I kissed you over two decades ago. And I'm still in love with you now." He slid his hand over her stomach. "This baby is just the icing on the cake."

The best kind of icing.

"So, what do you say about marrying—"

"Yes," Kendall answered before he even finished. And she gave him one of those delicious kisses. "Because I've been in love with you, too, since that first kiss."

More than two decades seemed like an awfully long time before they came to their senses, but he had plenty of sense now. Aiden pulled Kendall into his arms and held on, something he planned to do a lot for the rest of their lives together.

* * * * *

Find out the truth behind Whitt Braddock's murder when USA TODAY *bestselling author Delores Fossen's* SWEETWATER RANCH *miniseries comes to a gripping conclusion next month.*

Look for A LAWMAN'S JUSTICE wherever Harlequin Intrigue books and ebooks are sold!

COMING NEXT MONTH FROM

HARLEQUIN
INTRIGUE

Available July 21, 2015

#1581 A LAWMAN'S JUSTICE
Sweetwater Ranch • by Delores Fossen
Opposites attract when FBI special agent Seth Calder and journalist
Shelby Braddock stumble on a crime scene...and end up fighting to
survive. Their passion is strong enough to erase their pasts—if they can
evade a killer.

#1582 KANSAS CITY SECRETS
The Precinct: Cold Case • by Julie Miller
With his potential key witness's life jeopardized, detective Max Krolikowski
must keep Rosie March safe—and keep himself from falling for a woman
who could be a true innocent...or a killer waiting to strike again.

#1583 LOCK, STOCK AND McCULLEN
The Heroes of Horseshoe Creek • by Rita Herron
Sheriff Maddox McCullen vows to protect Rosie Worthington when
she turns to him for help. But can he ensure a future for them when a
desperate enemy wants to keep the secrets of her past buried?

#1584 THE PREGNANCY PLOT
Brothers in Arms: Retribution • by Carol Ericson
Assigned to protect Nina Moore and her unborn child, special ops agent
Jase Bennett poses as her fiancé. But when the charade begins to feel all
too real, Jase will need to risk everything to keep them safe...

#1585 TAMED
Corcoran Team: Bulletproof Bachelors
by HelenKay Dimon
Agent Shane Baker denied his attraction to his best friend's sister for
years. But when Makena Kingston's secret hobby puts her in danger,
Shane steps in to protect her—and discovers keeping his professional
distance will be nearly impossible...

#1586 COLORADO BODYGUARD
The Ranger Brigade • by Cindi Myers
Ranger Rand Knightbridge reluctantly offers to lead Sophie Montgomery
on her search for her missing sister. As the mission brings them closer,
ensuring a happy ending for Sophie is the only outcome he'll allow...

**YOU CAN FIND MORE INFORMATION ON UPCOMING HARLEQUIN® TITLES,
FREE EXCERPTS AND MORE AT WWW.HARLEQUIN.COM.**

HICNM0715

REQUEST YOUR FREE BOOKS!
2 FREE NOVELS PLUS 2 FREE GIFTS!

⊕ HARLEQUIN®

INTRIGUE

BREATHTAKING ROMANTIC SUSPENSE

YES! Please send me 2 FREE Harlequin® Intrigue novels and my 2 FREE gifts (gifts are worth about $10). After receiving them, if I don't wish to receive any more books, I can return the shipping statement marked "cancel." If I don't cancel, I will receive 6 brand-new novels every month and be billed just $4.74 per book in the U.S. or $5.49 per book in Canada. That's a savings of at least 12% off the cover price! It's quite a bargain! Shipping and handling is just 50¢ per book in the U.S. and 75¢ per book in Canada.* I understand that accepting the 2 free books and gifts places me under no obligation to buy anything. I can always return a shipment and cancel at any time. Even if I never buy another book, the two free books and gifts are mine to keep forever.

182/382 HDN GH3D

Name _____ (PLEASE PRINT) _____

Address _____ Apt. #

City _____ State/Prov. _____ Zip/Postal Code

Signature (If under 18, a parent or guardian must sign)

Mail to the **Reader Service**:
IN U.S.A.: P.O. Box 1867, Buffalo, NY 14240-1867
IN CANADA: P.O. Box 609, Fort Erie, Ontario L2A 5X3
**Are you a subscriber to Harlequin® Intrigue books
and want to receive the larger-print edition?
Call 1-800-873-8635 or visit www.ReaderService.com.**

* Terms and prices subject to change without notice. Prices do not include applicable taxes. Sales tax applicable in N.Y. Canadian residents will be charged applicable taxes. Offer not valid in Quebec. This offer is limited to one order per household. Not valid for current subscribers to Harlequin Intrigue books. All orders subject to credit approval. Credit or debit balances in a customer's account(s) may be offset by any other outstanding balance owed by or to the customer. Please allow 4 to 6 weeks for delivery. Offer available while quantities last.

Your Privacy—The Reader Service is committed to protecting your privacy. Our Privacy Policy is available online at www.ReaderService.com or upon request from the Reader Service.

We make a portion of our mailing list available to reputable third parties that offer products we believe may interest you. If you prefer that we not exchange your name with third parties, or if you wish to clarify or modify your communication preferences, please visit us at www.ReaderService.com/consumerschoice or write to us at Reader Service Preference Service, P.O. Box 9062, Buffalo, NY 14240-9062. Include your complete name and address.

HI15

"Did something scare you tonight...besides me?"

"You didn't scare me," she lied. Her fingers hovered in the air for a few seconds before she clasped them around the strap of her purse.

Max scraped his palm over the top of his head, willing his thoughts to clear. "Just answer the damn question."

She nodded.

She wasn't here for the man. She was here for the cop. He'd like to blame the booze that had lowered his inhibitions and done away with his common sense, but fuzzy headed or sober, he knew he'd crossed too many lines with Rosie March today. "I think this is where you slap my face and call me some rotten name."

Her eyes opened wide. "I wouldn't do that."

"No, I don't suppose a lady like you would."

Her lips were pink and slightly swollen from his beard stubble. Her hair was a sexy muss, and part of him wanted nothing more than to kiss her again, to bury his nose in her scent and see if she would wind her arms around his neck and align her body to his as neatly as their mouths had fit together. But she was hugging her arms around her waist instead of him, pressing that pretty mouth back into its tightly controlled line. When had he ever hauled off and kissed a woman like that? With her history, she'd probably been frightened by his behavior and had given him what she thought he wanted in hopes of appeasing him, counting the seconds until he let her slip away. She had to be terrified, desperate, to come to him after this morning's encounter. The fact that she wasn't running away from him right now had to be a testament to her strength—or just how desperate she was to have someone from KCPD believe in her. And for some reason she'd chosen him to be her hero.

Don't miss
KANSAS CITY SECRETS
by USA TODAY *bestselling author Julie Miller,*
available in August 2015 wherever
Harlequin Intrigue® books and ebooks are sold.

www.Harlequin.com

Love the Harlequin book you just read?

Your opinion matters.

Review this book on your favorite book site, review site, blog or your own social media properties and share your opinion with other readers!

Be sure to connect with us at:
Harlequin.com/Newsletters
Facebook.com/HarlequinBooks
Twitter.com/HarlequinBooks

HARLEQUIN®

A *Romance* FOR EVERY MOOD™

JUST CAN'T GET ENOUGH?

Join our social communities
and talk to us online.

You will have access to the latest
news on upcoming titles and special
promotions, but most importantly,
you can talk to other fans about your
favorite Harlequin reads.

Harlequin.com/Community

 Facebook.com/HarlequinBooks

Twitter.com/HarlequinBooks

 Pinterest.com/HarlequinBooks

HARLEQUIN®

A *Romance* FOR EVERY MOOD™

Stay up-to-date on all your
romance-reading news with the
Harlequin Shopping Guide,
featuring bestselling authors, exciting new
miniseries, books to watch and more!

The newest issue will be delivered right to you
with our compliments! There are 4 each year.

Signing up is easy.

EMAIL

ShoppingGuide@Harlequin.ca

WRITE TO US

HARLEQUIN BOOKS
Attention: Customer Service Department
P.O. Box 9057, Buffalo, NY 14269-9057

OR PHONE

1-800-873-8635 in the United States
1-888-343-9777 in Canada

Please allow 4-6 weeks for delivery of the first issue by mail.

THE WORLD IS BETTER WITH

Romance

Harlequin has everything from contemporary, passionate and heartwarming to suspenseful and inspirational stories.

Whatever your mood, we have a romance just for you!

Connect with us to find your next great read, special offers and more.

f /HarlequinBooks

🐦 @HarlequinBooks

www.HarlequinBlog.com

www.Harlequin.com/Newsletters

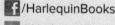

HARLEQUIN®

A *Romance* FOR EVERY MOOD™

www.Harlequin.com